CAUGHT UP IN THE LIFE 3

Lock Down Publications and Ca$h
Presents

Caught Up in the Life 3

A Novel by *Robert Baptiste*

Lock Down Publications
Po Box 944
Stockbridge, Ga 30281

Visit our website @
www.lockdownpublications.com

First Edition September 2020
Printed in the United States of America

Lock Down Publications
Like our page on Facebook: Lock Down Publications @
www.facebook.com/lockdownpublications.ldp
Cover design and layout by: **Dynasty Cover Me**
Book interior design by: **Shawn Walker**
Edited by: **Jill Alicea**

Stay Connected with Us!

Text **LOCKDOWN** to 22828 to stay up-to-date with new releases, sneak peaks, contests and more…

Thank you.

Submission Guideline.

Submit the first three chapters of your completed manuscript to ldpsubmissions@gmail.com, subject line: Your book's title. The manuscript must be in a .doc file and sent as an attachment. Document should be in Times New Roman, double spaced and in size 12 font. Also, provide your synopsis and full contact information. If sending multiple submissions, they must each be in a separate email.

Have a story but no way to send it electronically? You can still submit to LDP/Ca$h Presents. Send in the first three chapters, written or typed, of your completed manuscript to:

LDP: Submissions Dept
Po Box 944
Stockbridge, Ga 30281

DO NOT send original manuscript. Must be a duplicate.

Provide your synopsis and a cover letter containing your full contact information.

Thanks for considering LDP and Ca$h Presents.

PROLOGUE

After all the drama, I needed to move on. I had worn out my welcome in New Orleans. It was a great place to have fun in, but it had become too dangerous for me to live in. I had done too much dirt here. I had caused too much pain. I had to move on.

I pulled up to one of the company's condos, where I was supposed to meet my sister. I hadn't seen her in a couple of months. She had been crying for me to come kick it with her. She still didn't know the whole story about the hospital stay, and I wasn't going to tell her. If I were to do that, she would kill Shantel's ass for real. I needed her to run my company in New Orleans for me. There was nobody else that I trusted to take over. I had to spend more time with my family, especially now that Shantel was pregnant.

I glanced down at my phone and saw that I had missed a bunch of messages and calls from Shantel. She must have called when I was in the meeting with the mayor of the city closing the deal to build the new condos downtown in the city. It was a deal worth 100 million. I prayed the baby was all right.

As I dialed her number, I heard a couple gunshots. I felt a deep burning pain in my chest, legs, and arms as shattered glass covered my face and body. I saw the man with the gun. I lay back against the car seat, thinking that I had known that this shit with the cartel wasn't over.

My life passed before my eyes. There were moments of horrendous ugliness. I saw all the people I had killed and tortured. There were moments of sublime happiness. Shantell on our wedding day. The birth of my kids.

I heard my mother's voice. "Baby boy, you have to pay for the things you do. The past always catches up to you."

"Sir, hold on. Everything is under control."

I heard my sister screaming. "Please hold on, Keith! Please hold on!"

I could no longer make myself hold on. I tried to tell her it was too late, but I couldn't. I wanted to tell Keith Jr. and Ka'wine how much I loved them and how proud I was of them. I wanted to see my new baby. I guess it wasn't in the cards.

Everything went black. I flat-lined. The EMI's worked to bring me back.

With my last conscious thought, I thought about how I got in the game.

CHAPTER 1
Keith
Summer, 1989

I rushed out of school. It was my last day of middle school. I would be graduating to high school. I had to run. I had to catch Bruce before he left the projects. I needed to get some money from him.

As I walked in the Erato courtyard in the projects, I breathed a sigh of relief. Bruce was leaning against his all-white Mercedes. He was talking to this fine-ass chocolate chick with long red weave in her hair. She was wearing small, high shorts that her ass hung out of.

"What's up, Bruce?" I said as I approached him.

"Not much. What's good, li'l man?"

"Man, I need a few dollas."

Bruce was a big-time drug dealer in the Calliope Projects. He had grown up there, and he had a lock on the drug game in the projects. Basically he ran things back there.

I lived in the Calliope. They were built from red bricks and several streets ran through the projects. There were two sides to the projects: front town and back town. I stayed back town where everything went down: murders, drugs, and shoot outs.

Sometimes, a couple of friends and I hung out at the game room next to the Rose Tavern. We just liked watching all the fine-ass hoes and drug dealers. My mother didn't like me getting money from Bruce for two reasons. First, he dealt drugs. Second, she believed that he was involved with my father's death.

At one time, my father ran the projects, much like Bruce did now. One night, the police found him dead in his car behind the projects. He had been shot several times in his head and body. They didn't take anything from him but his life.

People in the projects say that Bruce paid someone to kill him so he could take over. But it didn't matter to me, so long as he gave me money.

Bruce reached in his pocket and pulled out a knot of money. He pulled out a couple of twenties and handed them to me.

"Thanks," I said.

"No problem. Don't tell your mother where you got it from. Look, Keith, when you're ready to get in the game, let me know."

"Okay, later."

***

I ran upstairs through the house to my room to change clothes.

"Boy, stop running through my damn house!" my mother screamed from the kitchen. She stopped me as I tried to run from the house. "Where's your ass going?"

"To the game room."

"No, you're not. Sit your ass down. We about to eat."

I sat with my mother and baby sister at the table eating red beans and rice with hot dogs in it. I swallowed my shit down because I needed to catch up with my friends at the game room. I swallowed my last bite. "Now can I go?"

"Yes, but take your sister with you."

"Do I have to?"

"Only if your ass wants to go."

"Okay, come on."

My sister and I had different daddies. Hers went to prison right after she was born for murder. He was serving a life sentence at Angola State Prison. My mother used to go see him, but she stopped. I guess she got tired of the long ride to get there. She still sent him a few dollars every now and then. He sent my sister cards, purse, and belts that he made in there.

Later on that night, Brad, Dave, Price, and I sat on the porch at my house and watched all the drug dealers hustling coke to make money for Bruce.

"When I'm grown up, I want to be just like him," I said.

"Me too," added Brad.

"Me three," Price said.

"Me four," Dave chimed in.

"Man, that nigga got all the hoes and money in the projects," I said.

“He sure do. And he’s always driving new cars,” Price said.

“And the nigga got lots of gold and diamond rings and chains on,” said Dave.

“Nigga, I wish I could hustle for him.”

“Boys, bring y’all asses in the house. It’s getting late.” Our mothers were paging us from their windows.

“I’ll catch y’all later,” I said, dapping them off.

CHAPTER 2
Keith
One month later

I was lying in bed when my mother snatched the covers off me.

"Keith, you need to get your ass up and go find a job for the summer."

"Mom, leave me alone." I pulled my covers back over my head.

"Your ass is going to do something around here. You're sixteen, and I'm not giving you money no more. I have enough trouble paying bills and taking care of your sister. You need to find a job so you can pay for your school clothes." She walked out, but returned a few minutes later, pulling the covers off again. "Nigga, get your black ass up! You're not going to lay in here and suck up all the air. This shit not free."

I got up, fussing a bit.

"Your ass going to do something." She stood with her hands on her hips, looking at me. Mother was a chubby red lady with freckles on her face. Her blonde and black hair was cut short. She looked like Tamela Mann, the gospel singer.

I put on a pair of black cutoff jeans, a white wife-beater, and some rundown Nikes that my next door neighbor gave me when her son went to jail. We lived on welfare. My mother got a couple of checks and went down to the welfare line to get the cheese, milk, cereal, and other stuff the government handed out. She also got her food stamps. After getting some food in the house, she spent the rest on cigarettes, beer, and going to the casino.

I looked at my brown-skinned body in the mirror with my ragged clothes and no haircut. I was tired of living this way. I was tired of chasing Bruce down for a few dollars. I needed to make some money of my own.

Niggas in the hood made money by fucking with Bruce. Them niggas got Bally's shoes and nice clothes. Some even got cars. I'm talking niggas younger than me. But I was just being stupid. I didn't want to fuck with him because my mother didn't want me to. She said fucking with him was going to get me one of two places: dead or in prison.

"Fuck this shit. It's time for me to get paid," I said to myself as I left the house.

I saw Bruce talking to this fine chick Rose. Rose was red-skinned and bowlegged with a big ass. She kept her black hair cut short. She worked as a stripper. I walked over to them.

"What's up, Keith?" Bruce greeted me.

"Man, I'm trying to get put down."

"You sure?"

"Yeah, I need to get paid. I'm tired of looking like this."

"Alright. Rose, I'm about to bounce. We'll get together later."

She rolled her eyes at me.

"Let's ride."

"Man, your girl tripping, huh?"

"Fuck that bitch. She ain't shit. She'll be on your dick when you start making money. So you want to live out your dope boy dreams?"

"If that's what you want to call it. I just want to get paid. I'm tired of looking like this and watching niggas younger than me get rich. I'm living poor as hell."

"Man, there's more to this shit than making money. What does your mother think about it?"

"Man, I don't even care at this point."

"Get in the car."

We got in his Benz. It was like another world. The seats were made of plush white leather. There were two twelve inch woofers in the back. He turner on the radio and "Paid in Full" by Eric B. and Rakim blasted through the speakers as we hit the interstate.

"You like that?" he asked.

"Hell yeah," I said, nodding my head to it. "Look, I need to get paid."

He turned down the music and looked at me. "Listen, li'l man, there's a lot more to the game than getting money. Once the money coming, problems always come with it."

I didn't care what Bruce was saying. I just needed money so I could buy my own Benz and some better clothes.

"Look, there's rules to this shit. It's more than just money, cars, clothes, and bitches. If you want to make it to the top and stay there, you need to remember some rules. Number five: be loyal to your people. Number four: don't trust nobody. Number three: don't use the shit you're selling. Number two: don't trust none of these hoes out here. The number one and the most important rule: don't under any circumstances rat on your niggas. You got it?"

"I understand."

"Good. Remember, this shit is always business. It's never personal. Oh yeah, and never fuck your man's girl without permission."

"I got it."

"Stick to those rules and you will get to the top in no time. Don't be like most of those clowns that work for me. They never save shit. They spend it all on bullshit. Stack your money and have something to show. One day, you will be as big as me. I fuck with you; that's why I'm telling you this shit. I want to see you make it."

We pulled up to a white apartment in the eastern part of New Orleans. The security guard at the gate let us in. Bruce knocked on the door.

A woman answered. "Who is it?" a tall yellow bone with long gold weave answered the door. She was wearing pink high shorts with her ass hanging out. She had on a light blue see-through T-shirt. You could see her hard nipples under it. She had a black gun in her hand.

"What's up, baby?" He kissed her as we entered.

"Nothing. Who is this li'l nigga?" she asked while looking me up and down.

"This is Keith, my li'l nigga. He's going to be working for me."

"Another one?"

"Keith is different. He listens."

"Whatever."

"Just go get me an ounce of crack."

I sat at the table in the kitchen and looked around the apartment. It was laid out with a big screen TV, white leather couch, and white carpet on the floor and a big fish tank with all kinds of fish in it.

"Man, you got a fly-ass apartment," I said.

"Nah, li'l man. This is a condo."

"What's the difference?"

"A condo costs more."

The woman returned with some grey high shorts on and a pink halter top. She put the ounce on the table. She sat down in front me with her legs spread wide open, showing me her pussy print. I wanted to reach out and touch it. My dick was hard as shit. I was staring so hard I didn't even hear Bruce call my name.

"It looks good, don't it?" he asked

"Man, I was…" I stuttered out.

"It okay, Kim wanted you to see that."

"Boy, Bruce, whatever." She got up and went to the back room.

Bruce unwrapped the ounce, took a razor, and broke a big piece off. "Look, this whole thing is an ounce, or 28 grams. You have four quarters in it, just like a dollar. Each quarter is worth $300. You can make $600 off of it. The whole thing is worth $1200."

"That's a lot of money," I said.

"Today, I'm going to give you a half ounce, which is…?"

"Two quarters and worth $600."

"You catch on fast. That's good." He sat there breaking it into small rocks. "These are called crack rocks. They sell for 10 and 20 dollars."

"Okay, I got it."

"I'll tell you what. I'm going to give you a whole ounce. Bring me 1200 and you keep what you make, which should be 1200."

"Okay."

He broke down the entire ounce and put it all in a plastic sandwich bag. "Here."

As I took it, his pager went off. He picked up his phone to return the call. "Okay, I'm on my way. Later." He hung up the phone and turned to me. "Come on, we got to go. Kim, I'm out."

She came from the back. "You coming back here tonight?"

"Yeah, I'll be home."

He dropped me off at the projects and smashed out. Before he left, he told one of his top workers to look out for me.

CHAPTER 3
Keith

I sat on the porch serving a few rock heads when my mother came out on the front porch fussing.

"Where the hell you been? I've been looking all over for your ass. I saw you get out of Bruce's car. What have I told you about hanging out with him?"

I had to make a choice either get money or continue to live fucked up. "Mom, I'm hustling now. I'm working for Bruce. You told me to bring money in the house."

"You can sell drugs if that's what you want, but you won't live in my house while you're doing it. So make your choice." She went upstairs and slammed the door.

At midnight, I was the only one still out selling rocks. I had about $100 in rocks left. I was sitting on my porch in the hallway as this fine-ass redbone crackhead named Trish came up.

"What's up, Keith. You got something?"

"Yeah, how much you got?"

"3."

"I don't have nothing for that."

"I could hook you up."

"What you talking about?" I was still a virgin and didn't understand. I was as green as a pool table.

"Come in the hallway. I'll show you."

In the dark hallway, she dropped to her knees, undid my pants, and pulled my dick out. It was as hard as a motherfucker. "Damn, you packing. Them hoes going to love you when you start fucking."

She slammed my dick to the back of her throat. She had my toes curling up my eyes rolling in the back in my head. I started shaking. I grabbed the back of her head, shooting all my nut in her mouth.

"Boy, fuck!" She pulled her head away from me, spitting all my cum out. I gave her a rock. She left the hallway, wiping her mouth.

I went up to my mother's apartment and smiled as I knocked on the door.

"Who is it?"

"Me."

"What you want?"

"Let me in."

She opened the door for me. "I hope you ain't brought any of that shit in my house."

"No." I walked in my room and fell into bed. I went to bed with a happy memory of the first time I got my dick sucked. I quickly fell asleep.

I was up early the next morning. I got a shower and fixed a bit of breakfast. My mother and sister were still sleeping, but I needed to catch Bruce so I could pay him.

I looked across the courtyard. He was leaning on his car collecting money from the niggas working for him. Bruce was brown-skinned, about 5'9" with black hair and waves with hazel eyes.

"Damn, Bruce. I see you got out here early."

"Yeah. Remember this, li'l man: the early bird gets the worm. That means the first nigga out here gets the money."

"Okay. Here's your money."

"Good looking."

"Bruce, why you out here selling dope when you got all the coke?" I asked.

"Well, even though I sell weight - quarters, ounces, ounces, half keys and keys - I need to watch what's going on in my hood. It's good to be hands on. Jump in the car."

In the car, he reached under the seat and pulled out two ounces and a quarter. He handed it to me. "Bring me back 3200."

"Okay."

He put it in a brown bag. I got out and ran upstairs to my room. I couldn't believe how much crack I had. I pulled out my shoebox and cut the ounces into rocks. I made my rocks bigger than everyone else's so I could get them off faster.

I went on an all-night flight, dying to sell all this shit. At some point it was down to me and my last customer. Two black guys I had never seen before ran up to me and pointed guns in my face. I froze. My heart was pounding a thousand beats a minute. I didn't know what to do. I thought I was going to shit on my pants. I was scared to death. I just prayed that they didn't kill my ass.

"Nigga, give me everything you got," one of them said.

I reached in my pocket and gave them all the money and dope I had. Half the money was for Bruce. I figured Bruce would kill my ass.

"Now get the fuck up the courtyard."

I ain't ran so fast in my life. When I got home, it felt like my heart was about to bust out of my chest. They had even fired a couple of shots in the air.

I called Bruce and told him what happened. A couple minutes later, he and some of his soldiers pulled up into the projects. They jumped from their cars with guns drawn.

"Where they at, li'l man?"

"They ran out the projects."

"What did they look like?"

"One was tall with nappy hair. The other was red with a low cut."

"Okay, from now on, keep this with you when you're out here. It's a .38."

The gun was black and brown and shot six times. It was the first time I had ever held a gun.

"They got some of the money and dope."

"Don't worry. In this game, you'll take some loses. It's just part of the game."

CHAPTER 4
Keith

The next day Bruce dropped off four-and-a-half ounces of cocaine. I had to get it rocked up on my own. I knew who cooked up crack for the whole project: Ms. Peaches. She lived a couple of buildings over. I knocked on her door.

"Who the fuck is it?" she hollered.

"Me. Keith."

She opened the door with a joint in her mouth. She was wearing tight brown shorts with a gray wife-beater and black Daniel Green slippers on. Her black hair was pulled back in curls. "What you want, li'l nigga?"

"I need you to rock this up for me." I pulled out the coke.

"Come in."

Her house smelled like weed. In her kitchen, she put the coke in a big clear tube along with some baking soda. She added water and put it over the stove. It was the first time I had seen somebody cook up coke.

Ms. Peaches was about forty years old. She was brown-skinned and slim. Her husband had been a big time drug dealer in the city until he got busted on the way back from Houston with twenty bricks. The Feds gave him twenty-five years. She cooked dope for everyone in the projects to make money to pay her bills and support her gambling habit. She liked fucking young drug dealers on their way up. She put her pussy on them and even let them hit her in the ass. She was trying to trap them. The last young nigga she had got busted and was sent to the state for ten years for dope and a gun.

She dropped a solid ball on the table along with a razor. "That's $100."

I handed it to her.

As she cooked the rest, I cut down rocks.

"Boy, I seen you coming up in the game."

"Yeah, something like that."

Someone knocked at the door. My heart started racing. I hoped it was not the police.

"Who is it?" she asked.

"Dawn."

I had forgotten that Ms. Peaches sold weed and crack herself. "What's good?" Ms. Peaches asked.

"I need a couple of dimes."

"Keith, give me two dimes."

"Damn. These motherfuckers are big. I'll be back," said Dawn.

"Alright."

***

I started moving work fast. Bruce was fronting me half bricks, and I was giving it to Peaches to cook for me. She kept wanting me to fuck her. As much as I wanted to, I had to keep it business.

I was trying to stack paper. I was helping my mother out with some of the bills and taking care of my little sister. My mother knew what the deal was. She told me to just be safe. I counted my money in the shoebox under my bed. I had forty grand saved.

It was time to get a car. My gear was right. I had Bally's and Polo everywhere. I was trying to get myself right for school and the back-to-school party. I was playing with a key of coke for myself, and Bruce was still fronting a nigga, so my pockets was good.

I took twenty-five grand and took a cab to Broad Street. There was a nine-eight I had my eyes on at a used car lot. It was still there. It was painted gray, but Price's brother could hook it up for me.

A bald white fat guy came out wearing a grey suit. "Can I help you?"

"I want this car."

"How old are you?"

"17," I lied.

"You have a license?"

"No."

"You'll need a co-signer. Come back with you mother."

"You're asking for ten grand. I'll give you thirteen grand right now."

"Okay, come on, we can work something out."

A few hours later, I drove off the lot with the car. I knew someone in the project who made fake licenses, so that wasn't a problem.

CHAPTER 5
Keith
August 1989

The back-to-school dance was finally here. It was being held at Fortier High School in the 13th Ward and them niggas up there be coming with it. So a nigga's gear had to be on point. I could have gone to Booker T. Washington in the hood. But I wanted to see different people and hoes. And besides, I had little cutie that went there and my friends did too.

Price's brother still hadn't delivered the car. I was getting impatient with this nigga. I was dressed fresh from head to toe. I was wearing black Bally pants with a red and black Bally shirt and belt. I had on black and brown Bally tennis shoes. My hair was freshly cut in a fade with waves swimming in it. I had on my big gold chain like LL Cool J and a couple diamond nugget rings.

As I was about to call him, I heard a car coming into the project beating hard. LL Cool J's "I'm Bad" was playing. I couldn't believe my eyes. It didn't look like the same car. It was painted pearl white with a white rag top and some gold Vogue Tyres on it. The windows were tinted dark. As Price's brother got out, I saw white leather seats and the twelve inch woofers hooked up to Sony Radio. The steering wheel was wood grain.

"Damn! You hooked this motherfucker up." I dapped him off.

"I take it you like it?"

"I love it." I gave him fifteen grand and jumped in the car and pulled off. I knew my shit was killing everything in the projects. None of these niggas hustling had a car hooked up like mine. When I pulled up at the dance, I was going to be killing everybody's shit out there.

At the school, all heads turned to look at me. I felt like a million bucks as the hoes and niggas came over jocking my car. Price, Brad, and Dave came out and dapped me off.

"Nigga, that motherfucker is clean," they said.

"Y'all like it? I told y'all I was coming to shut shit down."

"We see, nigga. You need to put us down with Bruce."

"Nigga, your mother would kill your ass if you start hustling."

"Nigga, we seventeen now. We in high school."

"I got y'all."

"For real?"

"Yeah, niggas. Let's go in this dance."

Inside the dance, my girlfriend Candy was waiting for me. We'd been dating for a couple months now. She was a high yellow mix of Creole and black. Her hair was running down her back, long and wavy. She was sexy and looked like Megan Good. We had never sex. She said she wasn't ready for all that yet. I wasn't tripping because I was smashing a few fine-ass crackheads.

She knew I had been selling drugs. She had asked me to stop. In fact, that was probably the major reason for us not having sex. But she didn't want to let me go either.

I had met Candy in the mall. She was window shopping at Victoria's Secret. I approached her and we started talking. I bought her the panties and bra set she was looking at. We went out on a couple dates. She stayed with her grandmother on Jean Street in the 13th, but her parents stayed in the eastern part of New Orleans.

"Hey, baby." She came over and kissed me.

"What's good? You look pretty."

"Thanks. Let's go dance."

We stayed until the dance ended at midnight. I drove her to her house in New Orleans East, the home of the rich and middle class. Her mother was a nurse while her father was a doctor. They had a big house on Lakefrost. We sat outside her house talking.

"I enjoyed myself tonight." She smiled.

"I did too."

"I like your car. A lot."

"Thanks. I paid a lot for it."

"Can I ask you something important? How long are you going to sell drugs?"

"Until I can get my mother out the hood and stack some money."

"What about me?"

"What do you mean?"

"If something were to happen, where would that leave me?"

"Nothing's going to happen to me."

"You can't know that."

My pager went off. A couple of niggas were trying to get something. "Look, I've got to go. I'll call you later."

"Okay, be safe." She kissed me.

***

A short while later, I pulled into the projects and ran up to Ms. Peaches' house. She was holding all my guns and dope, but I kept my money at my mother's house. If the police kicked in Peaches' house, they would get my money.

I knocked on her door. She opened it to reveal herself wearing small yellow shorts that had her pussy lips sticking out. Her hair was pulled back in a ponytail. She had on a pink see-through shirt and her nipples were standing at attention. I'm not going to lie, my dick was as hard as concrete.

"I need to get a couple of quarters. Niggas want some."

She walked over to me without a word and began tongue kissing me. I was nervous as hell. I had never been with a woman before. Well, okay, a few rock heads. But not a real woman. She led me back to the bedroom and took off her clothes. I looked at her big hairy pussy and her big titties. I couldn't believe this was happening.

She helped me out of my clothes. She dropped to her knees and started sucking my dick and balls. I was so on edge that my eyes rolled back in my head. My ass cheeks were tight. She got into the bed, busting her legs open. I climbed on top of her, easing my dick into her warm, wet pussy. I went to fucking the shit out of her.

"Fuck, yeah. Give me that dick. Fuck me." She was shaking and holding me tight.

She flipped over into a doggy-style position. I grabbed her ass and slammed my dick in and out of her wet pussy. She grabbed the sheet, screaming my name.

"Fuck, Keith! This dick is good!"

I began to shake and grabbed her ass cheeks tightly. "I'm about to nut."

"Yes, shoot it all in me."

I shot all my hot nut into her pussy. I fell back on the bed, trying to catch my breath.

"Boy, you fucked me so good. Like a grown man. And you got a big dick." She laid her head on my chest. As she dozed off to sleep, I eased from under her.

I got dressed, leaving her asleep. I grabbed the bag with the ounces, heading out the door to serve the clientele.

CHAPTER 6
Keith

As I was out in the courtyard hustling, this flame Brandy came up to me. At one time I wanted to fuck her, but the bitch wouldn't give a nigga no play when he was broke. Now that a nigga on, that bitch been all over my dick. She had caramel skin, was short with nice titties and a round ass. She had short red hair and favored the singer Melanie.

"What's up, Keith?" She was sucking on a Blow Pop.

"What's good?"

"You've been ducking me since you started getting money. I know you're around here fucking all these hoes."

"No. It's not like that."

"I'll tell you, ain't none of them hoes going to do it like me."

"I hear you."

Peaches came up and said, "What's good, Brandy?"

"Nothing. Keith, I'm going to holla at you later."

She left, and Peaches turned to me. "You better watch that hoe. She ain't no good."

"I hear you."

"I need some money and coke. I'm out."

"I'll go hit up Bruce." My pager went off. It was my girlfriend. "I'm going to fuck with you later on."

"Okay, let me know when it touch down."

"I got you."

I went over to my mother's house and called, "What's good?"

"I need to go shopping."

"Okay, I'll be there in thirty minutes." As I hung up, I thought that I should pick up a cell phone while I was at the mall.

***

Later, Candy and I were walking through the mall going into a bunch of stores. I bought her all brand name stuff, easily dropping ten grand on her. I bought myself some more gear and tennis shoes and a white cell phone.

"Are we still going to the concert?" she asked me.

"Yes, I got us tickets already."

"I love you," she said, kissing me.

"I love you back."

While in the food court, my pager went off. It was a customer. "I got to take you home."

As we sat there for a moment, she said, "Keith, I love you, but this…"

"Candy, I love you, but this feeds my family right now. Plus it's the way I just bought you all that stuff. But you're free to go. I won't be mad at you."

"Keith."

"I need to go. Hit me up later."

"I love you. I want to be with you. But this life…"

"I love you too, but this my life right now."

My pager beeped again. "This exactly what I'm talking about." She got out of the car slammed the door behind her.

As I pulled away, I returned Bruce's call. He answered, "What's good?"

"I need more coke."

"I'll meet you at the projects in an hour."

"Bet."

***

Later, Bruce came into Peaches' house with two bricks of cocaine. I had enough money that I didn't need to be fronted no more work. Plus, I needed to put my boys on. Bruce was really feeling them.

He charged thirty grand apiece for the keys. He took the keys out of the bag. They were wrapped in plastic and duct tape. "Here you go, my nigga. I'm glad to see you making moves. I told you if you followed the rules, you were going to come up."

I handed him his money in a black bag. As soon as he left, I called my boys.

***

Dave, Price, and Brad came over to Peaches' house. "Look, niggas, I got my own shit. This is two keys of coke. I'll front y'all some ounces so y'all can make your money. Peaches will rock up the coke for us. When you run out, come see me. That's how we gonna stay eating."

I gave all of them guns. I gave a .38 to Price and Dave, and gave Brad a 9mm. "So go get money, and bring it back here. We're going to be the young B.G. back here. Baby gangsters."

"We down with that," each of them said.

They watched as Peaches cooked up the coke. Then we broke it down. I gave each of them two ounces,

"Let's do this."

CHAPTER 7
Keith

We pulled up at the LakeFront area in our cars. I had my ninety-eight. Dave had a black Delta 88 sitting on Trues and Vogues. Price had a red ninety-eight with Disc and Vogues. Brad had a blue Delta 88 on some Disc and Vogues.

Candy was still mad at me. She wasn't speaking to me. Plus she told me she didn't want to come to the concert anymore.

The concert was packed. It was my birthday, so you knew I was about to get down. I was ready to ball out. A lot of rappers, including LL Cool J, Dough E. Fresh and the Get Fresh Crew, Salt N Pepa, and Public Enemy were appearing.

We stepped out with our Troop outfits on with the red Troop Adidas to match. We all were wearing Kangos on our heads and hitting gold chains and rings. We each had a pocket full of money and pagers and cell phones in our hands. We were balling out of control.

We walked into the arena. Bad bitches were everywhere. They had stacks in their heads and were wearing leather skirts with gold chains and medallion earrings. Niggas in there were fly too. When LL Cool J came out, the crowd went crazy. We rapped every song with him. Everybody wanted to be LL Cool J.

It was two in the morning when the concert ended. As we were leaving, Brandy came up with a couple of her friends. She had on a yellow leather skirt with a yellow and red shirt. She had on white Bally's shoes and gold medallion earrings. Her hair was dyed blonde in stacks.

"What's up, Keith?"

"Shit, chilling. You know today's a nigga's birthday."

"Yeah? You should let me break you off for your birthday." She smiled.

***

We went straight to the hotel. We got naked. She dropped to her knees and started sucking on my dick. I grabbed her head, stuffing my dick to the back of her throat as she swallowed it.

She got into bed doggy-style. I spread her ass cheeks as I slammed my dick in her wet pussy. She grabbed the sheets and looked back at me while I fucked the shit out of her. She came, shaking and screaming out my name. She climbed on top of me, bouncing her ass on my dick.

I grabbed her ass cheeks, slamming her pussy down on my dick. I started shaking as I gripped her ass cheeks even harder. "I'm about to nut."

"Me too."

She began riding my dick even harder. We came together. I shot my hot nut all in her pussy as she shot her cum all over my dick.

CHAPTER 8
Keith
Spring 1990

It had been a year. I had my shop and Peaches' house off the chain. I had Thalia Courtyard and Back Town locked up. I was paying a few hoes to hold some drugs and guns for me. I was getting six bricks at a time from Bruce. My niggas was doing their thing too. Everybody on the team was eating.

I was in my trap house with coke, guns, and money on the table. I was getting some head from Pumpkin, one of Brandy's friends. She had been blowing me ever since the day she saw me with Brandy at the concert. I had a handful of her red weave and was moving her head up and down on my dick.

"Fuck, you suck a good dick."

As I was about to bust my nut, the door crashed open. I thought it was the jack boys. I pushed her off of me and reached for my gun. Then I saw it was NOPD.

They rushed in, pushing me to the ground, showing their badges. I got on the floor with my hands up. They rushed over to put handcuffs on me. I was still under eighteen, so they couldn't charge me as an adult. They bought me to the juvenile building on drug and gun charges.

***

Two days later, I was in front of a judge for a bond hearing. My mother had hired a lawyer. I had been selling coke to an undercover officer. My mother and girlfriend were in the courtroom.

The fat black woman judge looked me over. "Keith Washington, you have been charged with distribution of cocaine and possession of a firearm while engaged in a felony. You're looking at juvenile life. Do you understand this?"

"Yes, ma'am."

"Your bond is set at $100,000."

"Yes, ma'am. Thank you, Your Honor."

My mother paid my bond. As I left the courtroom, my girl ran up to hug and kiss me.

***

We got to the new house I bought for my mother in Eastern New Orleans. I moved her out of the projects a while back. Fortunately, she kept some of my money in a safe at her house.

I jumped in the shower to wash the jail smell off me. Back in my room, Candy lay back with pink bra and panties.

"Come here, baby." She smiled.

"Baby, you don't have to do this."

"I want to."

I locked the door to my room and dropped my towel, showing her my hard dick. I got into bed, removing her bra and panties. I went down on her, eating her pussy out. Peaches had tricked me out of my head one night. She taught me how to eat pussy and make her cum.

I licked Candy on her pearl tongue. She moaned and grinded her pussy in my face. "Don't stop. Please, baby, I love you." She was shaking as she came.

I slid my dick in her wet, tight pussy. I eased into her as she tensed up and grabbed me tight. "Am I hurting you?"

"No." She closed her eyes tightly.

I stroked her slowly until she loosened up and starting humping me back. She grabbed me and pulled my face to hers, tongue kissing me as I stroked slowly.

"I love you, Keith."

"I love you back."

"I'm going to cum."

"Me too."

We came at the same time. We lay back in each other's arms as we caught our breaths. She raised up, looking at me, arms folded.

"What's wrong with you?"

"I told you this shit was going to happen, but you wouldn't listen!"

“Why you tripping?”

“Keith, there’s no telling how much time you are facing. You are going to leave me out here by myself.

“It’s going to be alright, Candy.”

“No, it’s not. You’re going to be in jail!” Candy jumped out of bed and put her clothes on.

“Chill out and lay back down.”

“Hell no! I’m out” Candy stated as she stormed out of the room.

CHAPTER 9
Keith

I called up Bruce and told him I needed him to front me some more work. I was down to my last twenty grand. When the police kicked the door in, they took four bricks and $100,000 from me.

While I was sitting in the courtyard, Bruce pulled up in his new black BMW, blowing his horn for me to come get in his car. I got in, dapping him off.

"What's good, my nigga?" he asked.

"Shit. My pockets hurting. I need to get put back on."

"I got you. There's a brick under the seat. I need twenty-six back."

"I got you."

I went to Peaches' house and knocked on the door. She opened it and hugged me.

"I'm so glad you're out. When did you get out?"

"A couple of days ago."

"What you need?"

"I need you to rock half this up. I need to get my money right before I go to jail."

"Jail?"

"Yeah, I'm out on bond."

"What did they say you're looking at?"

"Five years."

"Yeah? Damn! I'm sorry to hear that?"

I watched as she cooked half the brick. I broke it down into rocks and slabs. I grabbed a 9mm from her closet, took a couple of ounces, and hit the courtyard. I still had clientele. My boys had to start scoring from Bruce on their own until I got back on my feet.

Peaches and I sat on her porch smoking a joint as I sat there on an all-night flight. I stayed on that flight for two weeks. I just showered and ate on the run. I was about finished with the brick Bruce had given me.

I was serving a crackhead when I saw a man walking up the courtway wearing a black bandana on his face.

"Go inside," I told Peaches.

"What?"

I took my gun off my hip. As the nigga got closer, I went to busting at him.

He went to running. I shot him in the leg. He felt to the ground. I stood over him, emptying the clip into his face. I ran back to Peaches' house and beat on the door. She let me in.

"What happened?"

"I killed the nigga. Put this up." I handed her the gun. "I've got to go."

"Where you going?"

"I'll be back." I jumped in my car and pulled off. I called Candy.

"Hello," she answered.

"Baby, your people home?"

"No, they went out of town."

"I'm coming over."

"All right."

I parked a couple houses down. I crept to her back door, where she was waiting on me. We went to her bedroom.

"Damn, baby. Why are you sweating? You look strange."

"I just killed a nigga."

"What? Why?" She was staring at me.

"He was trying to rob me."

"Damn, Keith. This is why I want you to get out of the game."

"Not now, Candy, I got a lot on my mind. I don't need the preaching shit right now."

"Okay, you can stay here a week. My parents are on vacation. Now get out of them clothes."

I stayed over a couple of days, fucking the shit out of my girl.

***

I called Peaches. She answered on the first ring. "Where you at?"

"Safe. What's the latest news?"

"The police have been back here asking questions, but nobody is saying anything. When are you coming back?"

"I'll be through."

"Bye."

"What she said?" Candy asked.

"It all good. I got to go."

"Not until you give me some dick." She pulled me into bed, tongue kissing me.

***

Two days later, I returned to the projects. I had laid low at my mother's house, getting my shit in order. I had twenty grand saved up. I needed to go back to the projects and get the last couple of ounces and give Bruce the money I owed him. I needed to see Peaches too. I knew she wanted to get some dick out of a nigga before I went to jail.

I waited until it was night. I snuck back into the projects at one o'clock. Peaches answered her door wearing a see-through teddy and nothing else. In her bedroom, we fucked all night.

***

The next morning I grabbed my stuff and left. I met Bruce outside on the back driveway. I gave him a couple of ounces, $24,000, and my gun.

"Nigga, I'll be waiting on you when you get out." He dapped me off.

Brad and the rest of my friends pulled up in their cars.

"Nigga, be easy."

"We got you."

"Nigga, keep your head up in there," Price said.

"You know we going to hold it down out here," Dave said.

"I know." I dapped and hugged them niggas, then got in my car to pull off to my fate.

***

A few hours later, I was standing in front of the judge. My mother, my sister, and my girl were there. I knew I would be in there until I turned twenty-one. The prosecutor wasn't willing to deal.

"Mr. Washington, I hereby order you to be confined to the juvenile reform facility in Baton Rouge. I hope your time in Scottland will help you."

"I understand."

"I would advise you to use this time to get your life together and come out a better man."

"I will, Your Honor."

"I sure hope so."

They allowed me to hug my family before going back. My mother, my sister, and my girl all started crying.

"You be careful in there," my mother said.

"You know I got this."

"I'm going to be waiting on you. I love you," Candy told me.

"I love you back."

"I love you, big brother."

I love you too, little sister." I kissed her on the forehead.

The bailiff put handcuffs on me. I wanted to break down, but I knew I had to be strong. I couldn't show any weakness. I was going to jail.

I had heard about Scottland. It was a baby Angola. I had to put it down. No nigga was going to say I was a hoe in there. Not Keith. I had to represent my hood.

CHAPTER 10
Summer 1992

I had been in Scottland in Baton Rouge for two years. It was often called Baby Angola. Angola is one of the worst prisons in the state of Louisiana. Niggas get killed or fucked if they're not a man on the river. It's the same in here. You've got to be a little man. I've been in several fights here. You have to fight for a seat in the dorms, or your ass will be sitting on the floor like a lame. Niggas want to see if you can handle your business or if you will go out like a bitch.

I lost visitation and all my good time because I hit a nigga in the head with a weight. He had stolen something from my locker. I hadn't had a visit in two years because I had to keep fucking up niggas on the walk, usually over dumb shit. You can't let a nigga get away with nothing in here. I had to get my respect first.

I was in one of the worst dorms on the compound. It was called Maplewood. Niggas stay fucking and bucking the police, and they running in there pepper spraying everybody.

I was watching TV in my dorm. I finally heard my name called for a visit. I had gained a rep in this motherfucker. I had been pumping iron and eating right. A nigga was ripped up with washboard abs. I had grown to 6'1". I grabbed my new press up light blue pants and red shirt from under my bed where I kept them in plastic. I grabbed my all-black boots with the brown laces from under my bed and pulled them out of the plastic bag. I looked at myself in the bathroom mirror and brushed my waves.

I went to the gym for visitation. As I walked in, I saw my mother, my sister, and my girl. I hugged my mother as she cried in my arms. And then I hugged my sister. She had gotten taller and was filling out. Just like Candy. I hugged and kissed her. My girl had gotten thighs and an ass. I grabbed it as we continued to kiss.

"I love you, baby." She smiled at me.

"I love you back."

We sat down at the table to talk and to eat. I had received a couple of letters from my boys. Dave had caught a robbery charge. He got fifteen years in state. Price was dealing a little pot, but nothing major. Brad was taking hits on motherfuckers for money. Price and Brad had sent me a few dollars.

"Little sis, I see you filling out? Yeah, I'm sure your ass has got all them little boys running behind you. I ain't going to take care of any babies."

"Boy, ain't nobody doing nothing."

"Just be careful. Use protection."

"You're tripping."

"How you been in here?" my mother asked.

"You know me. I'm holding it down."

"You need to stop holding it down and come home."

"Well, Mama, it's about respect in here. If you ain't got that, you ain't got nothing. I'll die for it if I have to."

"Baby, listen to your mother and come home."

"I miss you too. I'm going to chill," I lied.

"You know, I start college this month," Candy said.

"Where you going?"

"Tulane. I'm going to be a lawyer."

"That's good. You can help me out."

"I know, right?"

They stayed a couple of hours. As they were leaving, my girl slid me $150. Money buys you things in here: good food, good soap, and everything else. I slid it into a cut in my pants. They searched you as you left.

"Boy, I put some money on your books. I sure hope this is your last time in jail," my mother said.

"Me too," added Candy.

"Don't worry about me coming back to jail. It's over with after this."

"Well, if you go back to that hustling shit, you're going on that river upstate next to your sister's daddy," my mother scolded.

"I hear you."

We took some pictures with the family. Most were with my girl. We hugged and kissed, and then I watched them leave.

***

I did chill out for my last three years. I finished my GED, and I even learned a couple of trades - not that I would ever use them. I just had to make my mother happy.

I had met this cool guy named Rick. He was from Houston, but had gotten arrested in Lake Charles. He was a young nigga trying to make money, like myself. He got busted with ten keys on the highway. I was getting out in a few days, and he wanted to talk to me. I was waiting for him outside the chow hall so we could go to the track and talk.

"What's up, Keith?" he asked, dapping me off.

"Nothing, nigga. Just waiting on your ass. You wanted to holla at me?"

"Yeah."

"About what?"

Rick was a high yellow, pretty nigga with cat eyes and good hair. He was about 5'6" and ripped. The nigga could fight. I had seen him knock out a couple of niggas playing with him. He had respect and like me, he had been down for the last five years.

He started, "Man, you know we're getting out around the same time. If you're going to try to do your thing again, we could hook up. I have a fire-ass connect with some Mexicans in Texas."

"A connect, huh?"

"Yeah, nigga. Cheap price."

"I hear you."

"I'll give you my number before you leave. If you serious about getting that paper, holla at me."

"I might just do that." I dapped him off.

CHAPTER 11
Keith
Summer of 1995

I got released on my 21st birthday. I told my mother and girl that I wanted to take the bus home. I got off the bus at the Greyhound depot across the street from the Melpomene Projects. My girl was waiting for me outside. She gave me a tongue kiss and hugged me tight.

"Baby, I'm glad you home."

"Me too."

We jumped in her white 5.0 and went straight to the hotel. As soon as we got in, we started undressing one another. I spread her legs and went down on her, eating her pussy out. She came back to back. She returned the favor by sucking on my dick. I could tell that she was just starting to learn because her teeth was getting in the way. I'd teach her better later.

I lay back, and she climbed on top of me and began riding my dick. I grabbed her by the ass cheeks, slamming her down on my dick. She came, digging her nails into my chest.

I flipped her over, hitting her from the back.

She grabbed the pillow and buried her face in the pillow, screaming, "Fuck, I missed this dick. Fuck, I love vou."

I started to shake and gripped her ass cheeks tighter. "I'm about to cum."

"Shoot it all in me. Give me that hot nut."

She backed her ass up on me, allowing me to shoot all my hot nut into her wet pussy as she came all over my dick.

We spent a couple of days at the hotel, fucking like dogs.

***

She drove me to my mother's house. I went in and hugged my mother and my sister.

"I'm glad you're home, son."

"Me too, big bro."

"What are you going to do now that you're out?" my mother asked.

"I don't know yet."

"I hope you got your mind right."

"Mama, you got the money?"

"Yes." She went to the safe and came back with ten grand.

"Thanks. Come on, Candy. Take me shopping."

I had sold my jewelry and car while I was in jail. My mother held on to some money for me. Of course, she spent some and sent me some.

Candy took me to the Plaza Mall. They had all the latest gear. All the stuff I wore back in the day came back around, like Louis Vuitton and Gucci. There were a few new brands like Prada. I grabbed new clothes and a couple pair of Nikes and Jordans. I spent almost everything I had.

Candy dropped me off at home. I needed to rest because I had to catch up with things. My partners needed to know I was home. And I had heard some things about Bruce that I hoped weren't true.

***

The next afternoon, I caught a cab to the Calliope, hoping to see Bruce. The nigga had changed his number on me. He had sent me money a couple of times.

I got out of the cab and walked in the courtyard. It was packed with people. They had this new thing they were doing in the projects called a DJ. Everybody from all over the city would come to your projects and party. I watched as hoes shook their asses to a new sound called bounce music. Soulja Slim was rocking it. Also, Cash Money was coming up and a nigga out of my projects named Master P had a song out called "Bout It Bout It".

Peaches saw me and ran up to hug and kiss me. She looked older and had gained some weight. "When did you get out?"

"A couple of days ago."

"Damn, boy. You sure look good to me."

"You too. Hey, have you seen Bruce?"

"His ass will be coming through here soon."

"What's he been on?"

"Snorting heroin, trying to maintain. And fucking and tricking to these young bitches in the projects."

Brandy saw me and ran over. She was shaking her ass to the beat in some tight pink shorts that was all in her ass. She tried to kiss me, but I moved my face.

"What's good, Keith? When did you get out?"

"A couple days ago."

"Your ass sure got fine. I would like to ride that dick sometime."

"I hear you."

I sat on Peaches' porch watching everybody party and all the hoes shaking their asses in small shorts as niggas watched.

Bruce pulled up in the project driving a black Jag with chrome rims on it. It don't look like the nigga was doing bad to me. He got out of his car wearing a fresh Polo outfit. He had a gold diamond crushed-out chain and diamond rings on.

***

Two days later, Bruce hit me up with a half brick and told me to bring him fifteen grand back.

I heard there was a new cooker in the project. After the police broke down Peaches' door a few times, she was done. Now all she did was turn tricks with old men. She turned me on to this new chick that stayed in the Thalia courtyard where we use to stay named Cookie.

I knocked on the door. She opened it and looked me up and down. "Who are you?"

"Keith. Peaches told me to come holla at you."

"Oh, you Dee Dee's son."

That's what they called my mother. It was short for Dana. "Yes."

Cookie was black and slim. She had short gold hair that was in a bob cut. She was wearing black shorts, a brown button-down shirt, and some brown Daniel Green slippers. She had a cigarette hanging from her lips. "What you got?"

"I need you to cook up this half brick for me."

"Come on in."

I sat at the kitchen table watching her break the half key down. I had heard through the projects that she liked to smoke Mo's - that is, rocks and weed. She put the first half in front of me to work on the rest. I went to work on it with my razor, breaking it down into $25 rocks and $50 slabs and bagged it up.

When she dropped the rest on the table, I broke her off a whole quarter. I watched as she rolled up a piece with weed and smoked it.

I took the drugs to Candy's car. She had let me borrow it. I made my rocks big. I needed to get my money right. As I started to sell, I saw a couple old crackheads I used to serve back in the day. When they saw me, they got happy.

"Keith, when you come home?" Marry asked.

"Couple of days ago."

Marry was an old crackhead. She had been out here smoking and tricking way before I got out here.

"What's up, Keith?" Charlie said.

"Nothing cool."

Charlie had been out here a long time too. He went to Angola back in the day for robberies, then came home and started smoking rocks. But I needed two motherfuckers on my team because I needed them to the spread the word for me.

"You back on?" they asked.

"You know it."

"Let me get a bump to get started. You know I'll run them to you," they said.

"Here," I handed them each a $50 slab.

"We got you."

A few minutes later, they were running vics to me. That was what we called crackheads. It went to bumping. I was serving them like a welfare line. I sold four and a half in less than a couple hours. Once the vics find out you got some good coke and big rocks, they coming running like roaches.

In a couple of days, I had Bruce's money and enough to get me a ride. Bruce knew a nigga that worked at an auction that could get me anything I wanted. Bruce and I went to the auction to watch the cars roll by. I wanted to get a Dodge Ram pickup. I saw a gray one with tinted windows on the auction floor. It had a couple of dents in it that I could get fixed. I could see it with chrome rims.

The bidding opened at $10,000. I had $15,000. If necessary, I would spend all of it. A coupled of others wanted it, but I outbid them at $13,500. I paid the auctioneer and drove off.

Back at Cookie's house, I took her the other half brick that Bruce had fronted me. I needed to get my truck hooked up for this get-together in the city called Super Sunday. Everybody got together to show off their shit. Niggas bring out their bikes, cars, and trucks along with their dogs, stunting for the hoes. Hoes be out there in their short shorts and halter tops with their hair and nails done, trying to catch baller niggas. This was where a lot of niggas were getting killed.

After she finished, I broke down some and kept the rest in quarters. Lots of niggas were buying quarter ounces from me. I was selling them cheap. They were going for $275. I was selling mine for $225. I had to rebuild my clientele. I had to get a couple of bricks of my own, so for me it was all about the quick flip.

When I walked out into the courtyard, crackheads ran up to me and a few niggas was waiting to get quarters from me. I sold everything quickly. My cell phone and pager were ringing off the hook.

CHAPTER 12
Keith

The next morning it was time to get ready for Super Sunday. For the event, I put on black Gucci shorts, a brown Gucci shirt, and brown Gucci loafers. I was wearing my gold chain with a big Jesus piece crushed out in yellow and red diamonds. I had a ring and watch that matched. I had a fresh fade. I sprayed on some Polo cologne and stuffed five grand in my pocket.

Super Sunday can happen anywhere in the city: uptown, downtown, or across the river. This Sunday it was downtown in the 7th at Honey Field.

I pulled up to the park in my gray Ram truck that was sitting on some twenty-four-inch chrome rims. The windows were tinted, and it had four twelve-inch woofers. I had on "How Ya Figga" from the new Soulja Slim album *The Dark Side*. I had niggas' and hoes' heads turning.

I parked under the Claiborne Bridge. I watched bad bitches walk by wearing short shorts and tight leggings. Niggas passed by stunting on their bikes or in their cars and trucks, trying to spit game at hoes.

As I was leaning on my truck, Brandy and Pumpkin came over. They were wearing matching white leggings and halter tops. Their hair was in crinkles.

"What's up, Keith? Your ass sure has been acting funny since you've been home."

"Your ass sure have," Pumpkin added.

"It ain't even like that," I defended myself.

"What's it like? You ain't even let me know you were home," Pumpkin said.

"I've been cooling. Trying to get this money."

"Is this your truck? When are you going to take us for a ride?" asked Brandy.

"You let me know," I said.

"I know you was fucking Pumpkin before you left. I'm not tripping on that. You can have us both."

"I'm down with that," Pumpkin said.

"I love to fuck a hot boy. Here's my number. Hit me up later," Brandy said.

***

As they walked off, Bruce came up on his red and chrome motorcycle. He had a bad yellow bitch on the back. She was wearing little shorts that showed off her ass cheeks.

"What's good, Keith? I see you shine."

"A little bit. I'm trying to reach your level."

"You will. I'll catch up with you later."

"A'ight."

I hollered at a few more hoes before driving to the lakefront, where the party continued. The new thing was to leave the park to the lake and to stop by the Daiquiri Shop on Crowder in Eastern New Orleans. After I left, I went to this club called Detour, a little hole in the wall uptown down the street from the Melpomene projects. It was jumping over the weekend. I saw Brandy and Pumpkin in the club, shaking their asses to some bounce music. I stayed a couple of hours, drinking and watching hoes shake their asses. Then I left with Brandy and Pumpkin.

***

At the hotel, I sat in a chair, watching them eat each other out. Both came over and grabbed my hands to lead me to the bed. I lay back and watched them taking turns sucking on my dick and balls. I couldn't believe that this shit was happening. Brandy mounted me as I ate Pumpkin out. Then they switched positions, taking turns riding my dick.

Both of them got into a doggy-style position, letting me hit them from the back. I was fucking Pumpkin as I finger fucked Brandy's asshole. Then I pulled out of Pumpkin and Brandy slid my dick into her asshole.

As I thrusted, I started shaking. I pulled my dick out, shooting all over their asses. I fell back on the bed to catch my breath.

They weren't done. They went back to sucking my dick, getting it hard again. I fucked them all night.

***

My cell phone woke me up. I saw the two hoes sleeping. *Damn, shit was wild as fuck last night*, I thought to myself.

I answered the phone as I headed to the bathroom. "What's up, Bruce?"

"You still trying to get two things?"

"Yeah."

"Meet me in the projects."

"I'll be there in an hour."

I slapped the hoes on their asses to wake them up.

"Man, what?" Brandy said.

"You want a ride? Let's go."

I dropped them off at the projects before going to the apartment in eastern New Orleans that I shared with my girlfriend.

CHAPTER 13
Keith

When I got home, Candy was sitting on the couch watching TV. She followed me fussing into the bedroom.

"Where have you been all night long? I thought something had happened to you."

"I'm good."

"Why didn't you come home last night? I bet you were out there fucking some hoes. I'm not going to keep putting up with this shit." She followed me into the bathroom.

"This is why I don't like coming here. Your ass is always fussing."

"I wouldn't fuss if you would spend time with me."

"How do you think bills get paid around this bitch? You ain't got no job. Your ass is going to school."

"All I'm asking is for your ass to come home at night."

I knew what this was about. I hadn't been giving her the dick like I used to. I'd been too busy chasing money. "So what do you want me to do?"

"Spend time with me," she said, getting in my face.

"I got you."

"Do you?"

I grabbed her and picked her up and carried her into the shower. I slammed my dick into her and fucked the shit out of her. I gave her what she wanted.

I got dressed afterward, leaving her sleeping.

***

I pulled into the projects. Bruce gave me two keys. I paid twenty-five apiece for them. I spent some time in Cookie's house bagging coke as she cooked down half a key. I had a couple niggas and hoes that liked that powder, so I had to bag some of that up too. Plus I was selling niggas quarters. When we finished, I left. I dropped one brick off at the house and took some ounces with me.

I had to make some drops to a few niggas that had hit me up.

I went to Bunker Hill in the eastern part of New Orleans. I had a few niggas there I was serving quarters to. Bunker Hill was a hood where niggas was thugging. There's a lot of abandoned houses, and niggas are making money.

I parked in front of this nigga Ro's house. He had it sewed up back here with the coke game. I met him through some mutual colleagues. He was short, brown-skinned with a big head. He was wearing some black shorts, a white wife-beater, and some black Air Max's.

"What's good, my nigga?" I dapped him off.

"Nothing. Trying to get this money."

"I feel that. What do you need?"

"A nine piece."

"It'll be 7600." I reached under the seat and gave him the brown bag. He gave me the money. I dapped him off and left.

As I drove away, I had more sales. Niggas and crackheads needed to score. I grabbed some more work from home and went to make a few more drops.

My phone rang. I didn't know the number, but decided to answer it anyway. "Who's this?"

"Me, Brad."

"What's good? Nigga, you ain't holla at me since I've been home."

"I know. I've been in the Parish jail fighting a murder charge."

"Where are you now?"

"I got out a couple of days ago."

"How did you get my number?"

"Shit, I came through the hood. I saw Brandy. She gave me your number."

"What's up with Price?"

"Last I heard he was in Hunt's prison. He got ten years for a drug charge."

"You straight?"

"No, that's why I'm calling. I can use a few dollars."

"Meet me at Rena's. I got you."

As I pulled up, I was thinking that shit went left after I got locked up. Shit got fucked up.

At the restaurant, Brad pulled in behind me in his red Dodge Ram sitting on eighteen-inch rims. Brad got out wearing Giraud blue jeans and a white Polo shirt. He had on white Polo boots as well. That nigga had gotten tall and big and he had shaved his head.

We hugged and dapped one another off. I was glad to see my best friend. It had been almost six years.

"What's good, my nigga?" I smiled at him.

"Man, chilling. You know, a nigga fresh out."

"I know how that feels. Let's go get some food."

Rena's is one of the best places to find soul food. As we were seated, the waitress took our order.

"What can I get y'all?"

I asked for a fried chicken plate. Brad got a burger and fries. We talked and caught up.

"Man, it seems like when I went to jail, you niggas fell off."

"That bitch-ass nigga Bruce wasn't trying to fuck with us. So a nigga had to make a living. David went to robbing them niggas that worked for him. Price sold weed. I went taking hits on niggas."

"Damn, my nigga. You got to give me them niggas' info so I can send them something. What you want to do?"

"To be real, I'm not with the drug selling shit. I'm about killing and jackin' niggas, for real."

"Well, Bruce is who put me in the game when I came home."

"Fuck that sucker-ass nigga. I really want to kill that fuck nigga."

"Damn, my nigga. Y'all beefing like that?"

"I just don't like the bitch-ass nigga. I think he's playing the game bad. I hear through the grapevine that he's back on heroin."

"Yeah, I was hearing that shit when I was locked up. But the nigga been breaking bread with me."

"Be careful. As soon as that nigga feels you're getting more money than him, he'll send his goons after you."

"That nigga knows not to fuck with me like that. I'd kill his ass."

"Just be careful."

"I feel you. Here's five stacks. I'm putting the team back together."

We left and I took Brad shopping at the mall. I saw Rick. I had been in prison with him. I walked over to him.

"What's up, Keith?"

"Nothing."

We hugged like long lost friends. He was in a gray striped suit with matching Gators. He was with a fine-ass redbone with a fat ass and long hair. You could see her curves through the light white jeans she had on.

"Man, what you doing in my city?"

"Doing some shopping. I'm here on business. What's up with you?"

"Nigga, chasing this money."

"Man, I've been waiting on you to hit me up about what I told you."

"I know. I forgot your number."

"Here. Put it in your phone."

"This is my man Brad."

"Nice to meet you. This my girl Wanda."

"Nice to meet you." I kissed her hand.

"I've got to push. Get with me. I'm telling you, it's all good."

They walked off.

"Who was that nigga?" Brad asked.

"He was a nigga I did time with. He might be my new plug."

"Shit, that's the nigga we need to be fucking with. Looks like that nigga really gets money."

"I'm chill. We'll be good."

CHAPTER 14
Keith
1998

My shop was booming. I was sitting in this bitch named Diamond's house getting my dick sucked, smoking on a blunt and watching *Scarface*. She was my side piece. She kept my work at her house in Kenner. The bitch was pretty, chocolate-skinned with short black hair and bowlegged. She looked like Keisha from the movie *Belly*.

I started fucking with her after she came home from prison after doing two years for boosting clothes. I took her shopping and got her an apartment. Once I fucked the shit out of her, I couldn't get rid of her. She does whatever I want. She knows about Candy, but she doesn't care. She loves how a nigga be treating her.

I had the project sewed up from Thalia Court to Earhart BLV. I was getting ten keys and paying for them myself. Bruce was still my plug. He was showing me some love on the prices. Candy and I were together, even though I was fully back in the game. She complained some, but when I gave her money and put the dick on her, it was all good. All she wanted was for me to fuck the shit out of her and spend some time with her.

My mother wasn't doing good. She'd been in and out of the hospital with cancer. I was taking care of my sister, who was starting high school. I bought her a Honda Accord for her birthday,

I started shaking. "I'm cumming," I said, shooting my cum in her mouth as she swallowed it all.

***

I pulled up to Hunt's Prison to pick up Price. Brad had given me Dave's information so I could get in touch with them. Dave had to serve 85% of his fifteen years since he was in for armed robbery. Price was making parole after seven years of a ten year sentence. He had to spend more time for stabbing and fighting motherfuckers.

I got out of the car as he walked out of prison. He was wearing prison blue jeans and shirt with brown boots. His hair was in braids.

The nigga got big. I ain't talking chubby either. He was built like the Incredible Hulk.

"Man, you look good, my nigga. Look like you used to lift the whole weight plow," I said.

"Something like that."

"Let go shopping."

I spent two stacks on him. We left the mall, and I took him to the Laffie Project in the 6th Ward to his girlfriend's house.

"Man, I'll pick you up tomorrow. We'll go buy you a car."

"Nigga, you rolling like that?"

"I'm all right. Here's three grand. Tomorrow, me, you, and Brad going to kick it like old times."

"Thanks again." He dapped me off and got out of the car.

***

The next day I took him to get a brand new car. I got him an all-black Camaro. We drove down to Copeland's on St. Charles to hook up with Brad. We sat at a table eating lobster and shrimp, talking shit and reminiscing.

"Nigga, remember when we were small. We all wanted to be like Bruce, having money and shit. Look at us. We made it. It's going to get better. I promise."

"Nigga, I need you to put me down. I need to eat on these streets."

"I got you. Chill. I'm going to throw you some work."

"Dave will be out soon. We all miss him."

"Let's toast to him." We raised our glasses. "To Dave."

My sister called me. When I answered, she was crying so hard. I couldn't hear nothing she said.

"Stop crying. Tell me what's going on."

But I already knew. The doctors said my mother's time was short. I knew she had passed.

"I'm on my way." I hung up.

"Is everything cool?" Price asked.

"Naw. It's my mother. She's dead."

"Wait. What's up, my nigga?" Brad asked.

"She been struggling with cancer. That was my sister. She dead."

"You want us to come with you?" they asked.

"I'm good. I need to go handle my sister."

"Let us know if you need us."

"Later."

I dropped them off and left the restaurant.

***

I walked into Universal Hospital. My sister and girl were waiting for me. My sister ran up and hugged me tight, crying. My girl did too. I was trying to be strong for them.

"I'm sorry, baby," Candy said.

"Thanks. What room is she in?"

"206."

I walked into the room, nervous and shaking. My mother was dead in the bed. Everything was neatly tucked in and she was covered in a sheet. I pulled it aside. She was small. Her black hair was thin. She didn't look like herself. My mother was gone.

I kissed her forehead. I cried a few tears, and then kissed her lips. "I love you. I got my sister. I promise you that."

***

The funeral was a week later. It cost twenty grand. I paid for it. All of my mother's family and friends were there. It was raining as if God himself was weeping. My sister and girl cried on my shoulder.

"I got us," I told them.

I spent the next few days with them. I gave the house to my sister.

But the game called. My grieving was over. Time to get back to the money.

CHAPTER 15
Keith

I had become the man in a few of the projects around here. I was supplying niggas. I was still scoring work from Bruce. I was getting fifteen bricks from him, but I was about to cut his ass off. His price - twenty-five a key - was getting too high.

Rick kept trying to get me on his team anyway. He was getting work from the Mexicans in Houston. But I wanted to be loyal to this nigga Bruce. He was on and off with the work. I needed someone to provide even in a drought. I had been waiting on him for a couple days, and he hadn't come through yet.

The nigga hadn't been looking the same. The coke had been shit. I'd gotten a lot of complaints about it. I didn't have time for that kind of shit. I picked up the phone and called him for the fourth time for the day. I didn't like sweating a nigga, but I was missing out on a lot of money because of his shit. No answer. I decided that enough was enough. I dialed Rick's number.

"What's up, nigga?" He answered on the first ring.

"Nigga, let's work."

"About time you joined the winning team. Come down to Houston."

"Nigga, I'm on my way."

***

I hit I-10 toward Houston. This was the first time I had been out of New Orleans of my own free will. It was time for a change. I needed to make moves on my own if I wanted to take over the city. That's what I really wanted. Fuck a couple of blocks. I wanted to be the King. This connect could get me there. Whoever didn't like it was going to get their ass rolled over.

I made it to Houston in about four-and-a-half hours. I called Rick as I made it in town.

"Nigga, I'm coming into town right now."

"Get off at the sign for Richmond. I'll meet you there."

I got off at Richmond, and he pulled beside my green Lexus in a black Ferrari F-355 Spider with chrome rims on it. I followed him into a bar called Scott Garlands. Damn, I never knew how big Houston was. You could fit a couple New Orleans into it. He was wearing black slacks, a white Gucci shirt, and black Gucci loafers. His hair was cut into a fade. He had on a small diamond and platinum chain and a Rolex. I was in some blue Guess jeans, green Polo shirt, and some black and green Air Max's.

I was jeweled up: big diamond chain, rings, and bracelet topped with my own Rolex.

"What's good? I'm glad you finally made it."

"Me too. Nigga, you're driving clean."

"Yeah, I paid $250,000 for it,"

"Damn, my nigga. You balling out of control. But you don't look like it."

"I don't want to look like it. I want to look like a businessman. People don't want to do business with you if you look like a drug dealer. If you look like a businessman, they'll kiss your ass to do business. Come on, let's sit at the table."

We sat at a table eating chicken wings. "What can you move in a month?"

"Shit, right now, I'm at ten a week."

"What are you paying?"

"Twenty-four or twenty-five a brick."

"Shit, he's killing you."

"I take it you can do better?"

"Way better. It depends on what you're getting."

"Let's say I start with thirty bricks a month."

"Eighteen a key."

"So the more I get, the cheaper the price?"

"Yeah, but you got to get them back yourself. If I take them, it's twenty a key."

"I'll have to see how I can get them back."

"I'll make the first couples runs at twenty until you figure out how you want to move them."

"You've got a deal."

"Is this your first time in Houston?"

"Yeah."

"We'll fix that. Come stay with me for a few days before you go back."

"Cool."

He lived in a suburb called Sugarland. There wasn't anything but mansions there. Rick had a big red brick house with a four car garage. This nigga was living large. The floors in the house were made of white marble. A large window overlooked the pool in the backyard. His living room was big. It had a large saltwater aquarium with sharks.

"Man, you living large. What did you pay?"

"It was 1.6 million. Five bedrooms with a pool and gym included."

"You're really eating off the dope game."

"You thought I was playing. I told you I wasn't. I've been telling you to get on the team."

A chocolate fine-ass bitch came down the stairs. She was wearing only a red thong and bra. Her hair was all the way down her back.

"Show him where he's sleeping."

"Damn, nigga, who's that?"

"One of my bitches I flew in from Hawaii."

***

Later we went to Jamaica Jamaica, a club in Southeast Houston. His all-gray Bentley had people's heads turning. He VIP-parked it. All the hoes thought we must be rap stars. He tipped the bouncer, who immediately let us in. We went straight to the VIP section. He ordered bottles of Armand de Brignac Ace of Spaces at $300 each.

The club was packed from wall to wall with fine-ass hoes that were thick and pretty. Several joined us in the VIP, shaking their asses to the new song by Juvenile, "Back That Ass Up."

We stayed until two and then went to an after-hours place called Cornbread. We left there with a couple of bad bitches. We went to his house and had a big ole orgy, and the beautiful Hawaiian chick joined in.

***

I awoke the next morning hung over. I looked at the fine-ass redbone lying beside me. I got up and walked to the restroom. I checked my messages. Candy had called a couple of times. I had told her I was going to Houston on business, but had forgotten to call her when I made it. She was probably worried.

I called her. “I’m sorry, I forgot to call. I was taking care of some business.”

“It’s okay. I wanted to make sure you were good.”

“It’s all good. How are you?”

“I have been throwing up.”

“You pregnant?”

“Might be. I’ve got a doctor’s appointment.”

“Keep me posted.”

“I will. Love you.”

“Love you back.”

“Don’t be fucking none of those hoes out there.”

“I got to go.”

I got in the shower. After I finished, I walked back in the bedroom. The Hawaiian chick was putting her clothes on. The bitch was super bad.

“Did you have fun last night?” she asked.

“I don’t even remember last night.”

“That means you had fun.”

“What’s your name?”

“Star. I’ve got to go. Hope I see you later.”

Rick put the girls in a cab. He had a maid make breakfast. We sat by the pool as we ate.

“How did you enjoy last night? Did you have fun?”

“Man, I can’t even remember.”

“You was off the chain.’

“I see.”

"I need to go handle some business. Make yourself comfortable. I'll be back. We can hit a couple strip clubs tonight."

He left, and I went straight back to bed. I didn't wake up until 9 p.m. I got up, showered, and Rick took me out. We went to a strip club called Harlem Nights on the north side of Houston. Every hoe in there was butt-ass naked and fine. He had to have twenty grand.

We left with a few hoes and had another big orgy at Rick's house. Everybody was fucking everybody. We had six bad hoes and watched them eat each other out. We took turns fucking.

***

The next evening, I got up, showered and packed my shit. I sat downstairs with Rick.

"I appreciate the love you showed me, but I need to get home."

"Anytime, my nigga. Just hit me up and let me know when you need that delivered."

"Will do."

We dapped, and I jumped in my truck, heading east on I-10.

CHAPTER 16
Keith

Two days later, I was at a storage room in the eastern part of New Orleans on Crowder Street at about one a.m. I was unloading forty bricks of cocaine on two pallets. Rick had some of his workers bring it in on a U-Haul. I had never seen so much cocaine in my life. It was pure snow white. No one knew it was there except for Rick's workers and me. I haven't even told my friends. That was the dope game, and the first rule was to trust no one. The forty keys on the pallet cost $600,000. I would make close to a million plus. I would have the cheapest prices in the city. It was all about the quick flip.

I grabbed ten keys and stuffed them into a black Gucci bag. Storage was prepaid for a year.

***

Back home, Candy was sleeping. The pregnancy test was positive. She was for sure pregnant. I was happy she was having my child, even if I was cheating on her in the streets. I wouldn't leave my girl for any of them hoes. I was going to get it together, but right now, I was doing me. I needed to buy us a house somewhere on the outskirts of the city. The condo couldn't be my safe house. I didn't like having my money and dope in the same house. If the police ran in my spot, I was hit. My girl had A-1 credit. I'd put everything in her name.

I put the coke in my safe with my gun and locked it. I took off my clothes and slid into bed beside her.

"I'm glad you made it home." She put her arm on me, never really waking up.

"I love you."

***

The next morning, I showered and threw on a blue Polo shirt with white Polo shorts and Polo tennis shoes. My phone rang.

"What's good?" I answered.

"Nigga, where you at?"

"Price? I'm on my way."

"Good."

We hung up and Candy came up with food and began feeding me. "Baby, can we go out tonight?" she asked.

"Where do you want to go?"

"They got Joe in concert at Tip A Tina's."

"We there. I need you to look for a house on the outskirts of the city today."

"Is this how you asking me to marry you?"

"I don't know about that. I just want you and the baby to be safe."

"I think you just don't want to give up on your hoes."

"On that note, I'm out."

"What's the price?"

"Doesn't matter."

"Okay, I'll just find something I like, right?"

"Something *we'll* like."

"I hear you." She kissed me and I walked out.

***

I stopped at the storage facility and then drove to the Laffie Projects off Claiborne in the 6th Ward. It was a big project and was painted an off-brown color. Niggas back here and in the 6^{th}in general sold nothing but coke. It's what the 6th Ward was known for.

Price was waiting for me on the porch when I got there. I grabbed the bag and went into the apartment. A slim red chick with short red hair was in the kitchen cooking pork chops and red beans.

"This is my girl, Tammy. This is my best friend, Keith."

"Nice to meet you,"

We exchange pleasantries. I pulled two bricks out and put them on the table. "I need forty-four grand back off them."

"I got you. Good looking out."

"Holla at me later."

I drove back over to the Calliope and Cookie's house with two bricks.

"Shit, nigga, I'm glad to see you back on. I thought you had quit," Cookie said.

"Naw, that dumb-ass nigga Bruce had me waiting for a couple days. That's over. I do my own thing now."

"Be careful. I've heard in the streets that the nigga doesn't like it when niggas take food out of his mouth. He puts hits on niggas' heads. He killed a few niggas in this city who stopped fucking with him."

"He knows not to mess with me. If he plays with me, his ass is going to get fucked over. Let's do this."

Cookie cooked up one brick. I weighed and broke down the other into powder quarters and ounces. I left the crack with Cookie and took the coke to Diamond's apartment. I had set her up in a project apartment. She sold quarters for me.

Now that I had coke again, niggas were hitting me left and right. I drove into Bunker Hill to meet Ro. He was waiting outside when I got there.

"What's good?" He dapped me off as he sat in my truck.

"Shit, coolin'."

"You got the money?"

"Yeah, twenty-two, like you told me."

I served a couple more niggas in the eastern part of the city, then went back uptown to a couple of niggas I was fucking with in the Magnolia Projects, the Melpomene Projects, and some interlaying neighbor hoods like Josephine and around Phillip and Clio Streets. Those niggas was copping four and a half ounces, nine ounces, and half keys and keys.

***

Later, I was in my kitchen running money through a counter when Candy came back.

"Baby, I found two houses that I like in Slidell."

"How much?"

She showed me the first picture. "This one is $250,000." Then the second one. "And this one is $350,000."

"Okay. Tomorrow, go to the bank. Get everything and put it your name."

"Which one you like?"

"The one you like that most."

"Okay, I'll do it tomorrow. Are we still going out?"

"Yes, as soon as I finish here."

"It looks like a whole lot of money."

"A quarter million."

"I'll get ready."

"I'll be right behind you."

I put rubber bands around the money and locked it in the safe. I undressed and joined her in the shower. I started kissing down her breasts and stomach. I went down on her, eating her pussy. I slid my dick into her as I kissed her and sucked on her neck. As I thrust in her, she moaned and wrapped her arms around my neck. I grabbed her ass cheeks and gripped them tightly as we came together.

***

Later, we pulled up to Tip A Tina's on Tchoupitoulas Street in uptown. The line stretched around the corner. We walked to the VIP entrance. Candy showed our tickets, and he let us in. We sat at the front table.

It was dark in the club. The only light was from candles on the tables. The atmosphere was elegant. Everyone was in white. I was in white linen. Candy was in a Louis Vuitton dress. We sat and watched Joe perform. We stayed until he left the stage.

We returned home and made love all night.

CHAPTER 17
Keith

Life had been good for the past three months. I moved my girl into a $350,000 house in Slidell. It was 3000 square feet with five bedrooms, a game room, and a pool. Candy was beginning to show. I went to a few doctor appointments with her.

I was getting seventy-five bricks a month now. My whole crew was doing well. We had all kinds of luxury cars.

I was getting ready for the New Year's party at the Warehouse, one of the hottest clubs in New Orleans. They were having the largest party in the city. I got dressed in white Gucci jeans and a brown and black button down Gucci shirt. I put on some black, brown, and white Gucci loafers decorated with gold buckles. I was wearing a white Gucci belt with a large gold company logo on it. I put on some Gucci cologne. My hair was cut in a fresh fade with waves swimming through them.

Candy was taking my sister out to see the fireworks before coming to the party. Everybody in the city was coming. Cash Money had just signed a $30 million deal and was going nationwide. Tonight would be popping.

I stuffed twenty grand in my pockets, ten in each. I put on platinum and blue diamond chains with matching bracelets, earring, and Rolex. All total, I had on a half million in jewelry. If a nigga robbed me tonight, he was going to get paid.

I drove to the club in a black Lamborghini Diablo Momo edition that had hit me for 350 grand. Price followed in a black Ferrari 380, and Brad in his black Corvette coupe. We were stunting like Cash Money and Bumping B.G. We had our shine on. Everybody in line was turning their heads to see who the niggas in the fly cars were. We all stepped out of our cars blinging with jewelry. I tipped the bouncer a hundred, and he let us in along with a few hoes that were on our dicks.

***

Shantell

I was in line outside the Warehouse with my friends Jackie and Kesha. Those hoes wanted to go to Cash Money's shit. I really don't care about that kind of shit. My mind was on college. I got accepted into the University of Houston, and had a scholarship to study business. I was ready to leave New Orleans. I was tired of all the killing. New Orleans was the murder capital. I was ready to meet some new people.

"Bitch, who are those niggas stepping out them cars?" Jackie asked.

"That's those niggas out of the Calliope: Keith, Price, and Brad," Kesha said.

"I'd like to rush one of them niggas," Jackie said.

"Who? Keith?" I asked.

"Bitch, the tall brown-skinned brother," Jackie said.

"I'll let them niggas run a train on me tonight," Kesha said.

"I feel you," Jackie add.

"Bitch, I'm going to see if they will let us in the club with them," Jackie said.

"No, Jackie. Bitch, I don't want to look all thirsty and shit," I said.

"Bitch, what the fuck are you talking about? The party's in there, and I'm trying to shake my ass and fuck with some ballers."

I watched as her ass walked over to them. She touched one of his friends on the arm and talked to him. I knew he was going to talk to her, because the bitch was wearing a black cat suit. She wasn't wearing underwear or a bra and had her ass and titties out, shaking everywhere.

"Come on. Let's go," she called back to us.

The club was packed with bad bitches and niggas. Cash Money was there and posted everywhere with the Hot Boys. They had bought out the bar for everyone. I stood at the bar watching Kesha and Jackie shaking their asses to the beat of Juvenile's "Back That Ass Up". Both came back to the bar carrying drinks,

"No, bitch. You're not about to chill. We 're going to get drunk and have a good time before you go to college for four years,"

Kesha said.

"Let's toast to us. To our long friendship," Jackie said.

The next thing I knew, I was drunk and shaking my ass on some nigga.

***

Keith

I watched from the VIP as bitches were shaking their asses off to Cash Money's records. We had made it a year without getting shot or going to jail. My whole crew was home except for Dave, but I had him when he got out.

"Let's make a toast to us," I said.

"To us."

We went out and got on some bitches. I was stunting harder than the Birdman himself. All kinds of bitches were on my partners and me. I was popping bottles all night – well, at least until Candy and my sister came in. At that point, I had to turn it down.

She came up to me in the VIP section. "'Hey, baby." She kissed me in the mouth in front of the hoes in there. She was like a lion marking her territory. She was waiting for one of those hoes to say something, pregnant and all. They just smiled and left.

"What's good?" I asked.

"Nothing. I just came by to kick it with you."

"I'm cool with that. I wouldn't have it any other way."

"They're starting the countdown."

Everybody picked up a glass as we counted down. "Five, four, three, two, one. Happy New Year's."

"We made it into 1999." I kissed Candy and hugged my sister and crew.

We partied and drank until the club closed at sun-up. I went home and made love to Candy.

My phone woke me up. It was niggas looking for coke. The clock showed noon. I had a hangover. I laid my ass back down and fell asleep.

CHAPTER 18
Shantel
Summer 1999

"Bitch, we're going to miss you." Jackie and Kesha gave me a group hug.

"I'ma miss y'all."

I turned to my mother. I hugged her and tears poured down our faces. "I'm so proud of you. I love you."

"I love you too." I kissed her on the cheek.

"Call if you need anything."

"I will."

I got in my red Honda Accord. My mother had bought it for me when I finished high school. Everything was packed and in the car. I got out and hugged everyone again. I got in my car and drove away. I'm not going to lie. As much as I wanted to leave New Orleans, a big part of me wanted to stay. Houston was nothing like New Orleans, like home. I heard places closed early, plus there was no soul food - no gumbo or po'boy's.

I watched my childhood friends as they receded in my mirror. I shed a few tears when I got on I-10 to Houston. I didn't know if I could adjust to a city that large.

***

The trip to Houston took four-and-a-half hours. As I pulled into town, I could see a large skyscraper made entirely of glass. It was the Hyatt-Regency building, but I didn't know that then.

I got off 610 and drove over to the university, which was mainly red brick buildings. I got out and headed to my dorm room with a lot of my stuff. In the room, my new roommate was already there. She had brown skin, was thick, and had short black hair. She was wearing some tight white jeans that showed off her round, fat ass. A halter top held her nice-sized titties in place. She was hanging pictures of different Houston rappers.

"I'm sorry. I didn't hear you come in." She smiled.

"It's cool. I'm Shantel."

"I'm Brittney. Where are you from?"

"New Orleans."

"I can tell by the way you talk. Y'all's accent is different from anybody else in the world."

"Where are you from?"

"Houston."

I dropped my stuff on the bed and went back to grab the rest of my stuff. As I got back, she asked, "What's your major?"

"Business."

"Me too."

"Well, it looks like we'll be both class and roommates."

"Is this your first time in Houston?"

"Yes."

"I'll show you around the city. We'll have a good time."

"Okay."

"There's a party at the club tonight. Do you want to come?"

"Sure, why not?"

CHAPTER 19
Keith

I was balling so hard with my new plug that I was thinking about taking over some of the other projects. This nigga Charles was running the Magnolia, Craig had the Melpomene on lock, and Bird controlled the St. Thomas. Those niggas' prices were too high. I had the cheapest coke in the city.

Bruce had been calling and saying that we needed to talk. Diamond, Brandy, and Pumpkin, were on the team. They were transporting keys of coke to New Orleans. I bought cars with stash spots that could handle 100 keys each. I wanted to move up to 400 keys because 100 lasted less than a month.

Price was flooding the 6th, 7th, and 8th Wards with coke. Even though Brad said he didn't want to move anything, he was in on it and pushing keys though the 9th Ward.

I was in my white Benz 603 S1 with a slim redbone with short blond and black hair. I had gone to school with Trish; she'd been trying to hook up with me for a while. But she warned me that she was the police: NOPD. I had thought that she was trying to set me up, but it turned out she was corrupt and wanted to be paid. We fucked a few times, but her main value was that she warned me when raids were about to come down.

Bruce called me. "We need to talk."

"I'll meet you in the project in thirty minutes."

"Baby, I thought we were spending time together?" Trish said.

"I have to handle this. I'll be back later."

"You promise?"

"Yeah."

She kissed me before getting out of the car.

***

When I got to the project, Bruce and his crew were leaning against his car. The shit didn't look right, so I grabbed my .45 and stuck it on my hip. Bruce's problem is that he has to be in charge.

Since I'm scoring from someone else and he's not getting a cut, he's got a problem. He's not eating on the streets like he used to. His coke is trash. The shit's been stepped on a thousand times. He needs to learn that he's not operating the only candy store in town.

I walked over to him. "What's good?" I dapped him off.

"Nothing's good. It's all bad when I have to find out from the streets that you are the Keith that everybody is talking about. The one with the cheaper coke prices. The family isn't getting a cut either."

"I'm looking out for my family. My crew."

"Is that right? I hear you got a new plug. You're pushing a lot of weight."

"Yeah, something like that."

"You want to turn me onto the plug?"

"Naw, it's not going to work like that."

"Nigga, this is how it's going to be after all I did for you? Nigga, I put you in the game."

"And I appreciate it."

"I can tell you don't want to put a nigga down."

"You can score from me."

"And who is you? I do my own thing."

"Well, you can take it or leave it."

"I'm going to leave it." He got in my face.

I pushed him away. "Man, watch out." I had my hand on my strap. I got in my car and pulled off.

It was bad blood between us now. I knew I was going to have to kill this nigga.

***

Shantell

We were going to Connection's, a club in the southeast, in Brittney's red Benz. The line was wrapped around the corner. We had been going out since I first got here six months ago. She took me out everywhere to show me the city. This motherfucking city is as big as fuck. You would get lost if you didn't know where you were going.

I had been smoking weed and drinking like a motherfucker every night. This bitch had shown me love and turned me out. I didn't have to pay for shit. She always had stacks of money. She knew everyone. They respected her in Houston.

Brittney and I had grown really close. The bitch was cool as fuck. School, however, wasn't going so well. I'd missed a lot of classes. They were talking about taking my scholarship. I had to get my shit together - but not tonight.

We were both wearing Prada. For me, tight blue jeans, a red shirt, and stilettos. I was carrying a white purse that cost $2500. Brittney had brought it for me. We had driven to Lake Charles. I don't know what she did there, but we stayed a week, and she came back with a lot of money. Besides the purse, she gave me a thousand dollars.

Brittney had on white jeans and stiletto boots with a yellow shirt. She was also carrying a white purse. Our hair was freshly permed and hung down to the middle of our backs. There were baller niggas outside the club with their old school rides. In Houston, they called it parking lot pimping. A few tried to holla at us, but we ignored them.

I didn't fuck with anyone up here yet. I hadn't found a nigga I liked. Lord knows I needed some dick. My pussy was on fire. I would give my old boyfriend some, but he had gotten five years in jail for drugs.

Brittney tipped the bouncer and we went in to the VIP. She ordered bottles of Remy Martin. The club was big and had a large dance floor, a big DJ booth, and two bars. There were fines hoes and good-looking niggas. It was off the chain. They were playing music by Cash Money as well as Houston rapper Mike Jones.

Brittney grabbed me and dragged me to the dance floor. "I don't come here to look. I came to have fun."

We shook our asses on one another as well as on other niggas. We stayed until it closed. We left tipsy and high on weed.

We got back to the campus at three in the morning. We were

smoking weed on the couch. When she kissed me, I thought I was tripping at first, but she kissed me again and started rubbing my pussy. I didn't know what to do. I had never been with a girl before. I wanted to stop her, but I needed to get off. My pussy was on fire.

She took off my bra and pushed me onto the bed. She sucked my hard red nipples as I lay there moaning. She took off my jeans and thong at the same time. She kissed me on the stomach as she made her way to my pussy. I exhaled deeply. I was glad I had shaved my pussy.

She kept licking my pussy lips as I moaned. I grabbed a handful of her hair and held her head tightly in place as she licked and sucked on my clit. I came all in her mouth. It was the first time I came back to back.

She rimmed my asshole with her tongue. I came back to back again.

She stripped and taught me how to please her. I did the same to her as she did for me. We came so much that we fell in my bed.

From that point on, I was into both women and men. I was bisexual. That wouldn't be my last experience. I had been exposed to something new, and I liked it.

CHAPTER 20
Keith

"Fuck yeah, daddy, give me that dick," Trish said, looking back at me and biting on her lips.

I was fucking her doggy style and was playing with her ass with a finger while I fucked her pussy. She was a big freak. She liked it in the ass. Her boyfriend, a fellow police officer, was lame. She was a good girl and liked thug niggas.

I slammed my dick in her asshole. I grabbed her ass cheeks, fucking her like she wanted it. I began to shake. "I'm going to nut."

She pulled my dick out of her ass and swallowed my dick, letting me cum in her mouth. I fell back on the bed, trying desperately to catch my breath. She sucked my dick back to full hardness. She got on top of me in a reverse cowgirl position.

"Fuck, I love this dick. And I love you." She was shaking and cumming again.

I flipped her over, put her legs on my shoulders, and went to beating her out like DMX did Keisha in *Belly*, my favorite movie.

"Fuck this pussy. Give me that dick." Her fingernails dug into my back.

"Fuck, I'm about to nut."

She held me tighter and wrapped her legs around me as I shot my hot nut into her super wet pussy.

"Fuck, boy, I swear I love you. I'm thinking of leaving that nigga for you."

But it was the dick talking to her. She always said that after I dropped my dick in her and had her cumming out of her mind. Then she came to her senses. She had four kids with him. I'm a drug dealer.

I left her in the bed to fall asleep. I put on some shorts and grabbed a blunt. In the kitchen, I had money and six keys on the table. I had to count the money so I could re-up again.

***

I hadn't been in the projects in weeks. I was too busy running all over the city selling keys. I had the projects on lock. My clientele was through the roof. I had the cheapest prices in the city. Niggas came from all over to buy from me.

I was coming back across the river from delivering when I decided I needed to stop by the projects. It would be a good idea to go in the projects to see how shit was moving and check a few trap spots.

As soon as I turned in, a hail of bullets rained down on my car. A couple of bullets broke the glass, hitting my shoulder. I swerved, hitting a parked car. I could still move, but blood was everywhere. All I could see was niggas running toward me. I closed my eyes to pray. A woman screamed. I passed out.

***

Sometime later, I woke up in the hospital. I didn't know why I was there, or how I got there. I vaguely remembered hitting a parked car.

Candy was sitting in a chair watching me. Tubes were everywhere. I couldn't move.

"Shh, baby. Don't try to talk. I'm here." She was holding my hand.

The doctor came in to remove the ventilator tube. I tried to speak, but my mouth was too dry. Candy held water to let me sip it.

"What happened?" I croaked.

"You were shot and ran into a parked car," the doctor replied.

"Damn, that's why I hurt."

"I'll get you some meds. You need to get some rest."

"How long will I be here?"

"Until I say you can go. We need to run tests, and you need rest." He left.

After he left, Candy asked, "Do we need to leave the city?"

"Why are you asking that?"

"People trying to kill you."

"I'm not going anywhere. I'm going to get my respect. Ain't nobody going to run me from my city. Ain't no nigga going to shoot me and get away with it. I ain't no hoe. These my streets."

"Next time, you might not be so lucky."

"You're right. I'm going to find out who did this shit and kill their ass."

"Okay, I'll do whatever you want."

"Have Brad and Price come by?"

"Yeah. They were here earlier when you were sleeping.

"I'm going to have a junior and give him my name."

"That's a lie. My baby ain't getting caught up in this bullshit as street life. He's going to be a square and go to college."

"I hear you."

I lay back on the bed, thinking about this shit. I had a lot of niggas hating on me because I was either taking their clientele or fucking their bitch. But no worries. I was going to find out who was behind this.

***

A month elapsed before they let me out of the hospital. I was still sore, so Candy had me on bed rest. While she took care of me. Price and Brad were holding everything down in the streets. I put some money on a nigga's head to anyone who could tell me who shot me. I thought it was most likely Bruce, but I needed more proof. Brad was searching for him. Brad would kill him if he caught him slipping.

I called my plug to let him know I was coming. I was down to my last fifty keys. I needed to score some more, at least 600 keys. We needed to negotiate the price. I needed to get them for thirteen to fifteen now that I was buying so many.

Rick answered, and I started. "Man, what's good on the work?"

"How are you?"

"I'm good. A little sore, but know I'm a G. We need to talk prices."

"Cool. Come on down."

"See you soon."

I got out of bed as Candy came back in the room.

"What are you doing out of bed?"

"I need to shower. I need to make a move to Houston."

"You're not well."

"I'm straight. I need to handle business."

"Baby, you need to slow down." '

"I got this." My phone rang. "What's good, Brad?"

"Man, I just smashed one of that nigga Bruce's people."

"Where at?"

"Around the car wash on Claiborne."

"Bruce?"

"He wasn't with him."

"Keep your head up. I need to make a run out of town. I need you and Price to keep and eyes on Candy."

"I got you. Later."

As I hung up, Candy said, "I don't need no babysitter. I'm a grown-ass woman. I can take care of myself."

"Brad just killed one of Bruce's people. I need you to be cool right now. You do that for me?"

"Yes."

If you need to go anywhere, let Brad or Price take you."

I took a shower and took off for Houston.

CHAPTER 21
Keith

As I left the airport, Rick was waiting for me in a black Cadillac Escalade. As his driver opened the door, I saw Rick was wearing an all-white LV suit and loafers.

"I'll deal with this later. I'll call you back in an hour." He hung up his phone and turned to me. "How are you doing?"

"I'm fine. You know me. It's all business to me."

"I'm glad to see you. When was the last time you went out?"

"It's been a minute."

"We're gon' have some fun while you're here."

"I'm really here on business, you know."

"It's always business, but no fun ain't no good. Enjoy the fruits of your labor. Why make money if you're not going to spend it?"

"You're right."

We pulled up to a big white house in Houston's Museum district.

"Man, I see you came up and moved around."

"Yeah, this is where rich whites stay." This house was bigger and nicer than the last one. "I paid 2.4 million for it. Six bedrooms with five full baths and two half-baths. There's a pool out back, a game room, elevator, and four car garage.

"Man, this motherfucker is nice. I need to move out here."

"Houston's big enough for both of us."

"Remember back in juvie, you talked about us hooking up."

"And your ass took so long."

"You know, but now we're millionaires."

"You know it."

***

We went to a strip club on the northside called Harlem Nights. We were in his gray Rolls Royce convertible with the top down. It was Friday night and it was packed. All the niggas were outside showing off their cars, trucks, and bikes. My favorite thing about

Houston: niggas were getting real money. There wasn't none of that hating shit like New Orleans. Here, a lot of niggas were players. Everybody was eating, for real. In the city, niggas wanted to kill you if you were shining.

We got out of his car clean as a motherfucker. I was wearing all Gucci: brown pants, a red and brown shirt, a gold and black belt, and black and brown boots. I was iced out with $250,000 in jewelry. Rick was in Louis Vuitton: grey slacks and shirt with black loafers.

We went straight into the club. They knew Rick in the city. At the bar, Rick got twenty thousands in ones. We got shot glasses and a bottle of Patron. We went to the front right and sat there drinking shots and throwing money. A couple of redbones with long hair and tattoos on their asses, a couple of black chicks, and some Spanish hoes gave us lap dances. Bitches everywhere were butt-naked. Back home, it was just topless.

We kept drinking shots and throwing money. Rick spent every bit of $50,000 in there. We left the club with a couple of them hoes and took them back to Rick's house. I took a redbone and black Mexican upstairs. As soon as we hit the room, we all took off our clothes. They took turns sucking my dick. One sucked my balls while the other sucked my dick.

The redbone started eating out the Mexican chick from behind. Red climbed on top of me, riding my dick as the Mexican chick sucked her titties. They switched positions, then they got in a doggy-style position and let me hit them from the back. As I was about to cum, they moved to let me shoot my nut in their faces. I fell back on the bed and felt one sucking my dick back to hardness.

They fucked the shit out of me all night.

***

The next evening, Rick and I sat at Red Lobster while we talked business.

"You need more keys?" Rick asked.

"Yeah, 600 a month. But the price needs to go down."

"What're you wanting to pay?"

"13.5 a key."

"13.5 a key?"

"I bring it in myself. I got people I need to pay too."

"Let me think about it."

"My nigga, I move 400 keys in less than two months."

"I didn't say no. I just said let me think about it. When are you leaving?"

"A couple of days. I need to get back to my city. I got some niggas hating on my shit."

"Do you think you'll be alive to move this shit?"

"Yeah, don't worry about that."

"Keith, don't take this war shit lightly."

"I'm not. I got this."

"Okay. Now, we're going out tonight."

"Nigga, you party like a motherfucker."

"I'm enjoying my life. I make money to enjoy it. When I'm gone, somebody else will enjoy it."

"I feel you."

"You got kids?"

"Naw, but my girl's expecting. You?"

"Four boys and two girls."

"I'm having a boy."

"That's good. Boys are better than girls. Come on; let's get out of here."

***

We went back to Jamaica Jamaica. It was off the chain! Bad bitches were shaking their asses on the dance floor. We went to the VIP and ordered bottles of Ace of Spades, the shit that Jay Z kept talking about.

A couple of hoes joined us. The one sitting on my lap was half-black and half-Mexican. She was in tight red jeans, a black blouse, and red stilettos. Her hair was blue and hung down to her shoulders.

"I'm Stephanie. What's up, daddy?"

"I'm Keith."

"You sound like you're from New Orleans."

"I am."

"How long are you in town for?"

"A couple of days."

"Come on; let's go on the dance floor."

I told Rick I was going to be back. We hit the dance floor, and she started shaking her ass off on me to Juvenile's "Back That Ass Up". I got behind her, grinding my dick into her ass. When my dick got rock hard, she grinded it even harder.

Later, we went back to the VIP to have a couple drinks. "So, what are you getting into after the club?" she asked.

"Shit, hopefully you."

We stayed until the club closed and then went to this club called Coinbread, an after-hours spot. The hoes followed us. After chilling for a couple of hours, I took her back to Rick's house.

As soon as we got in, she took off her clothes. Her body was right with no marks on it. She pushed me back on the bed and swallowed my whole dick. She deep-throated it like a pro. She climbed on top of me and started riding my dick. I grabbed her ass cheeks and slammed her down on top of my dick.

"Fuck, yeah. Ride that big dick."

"Fuck, I'm cumming!" she cried out.

I flipped her over in a doggy-style position and spread her ass cheeks, gripping them as I rammed my dick in her pussy.

"Fuck yeah," she moaned, "I'm cumming."

"I'm about to nut."

I pulled my dick out of her, shooting nut all over her ass cheeks and back.

CHAPTER 22
Keith

The next morning I woke to my cell phone ringing. I looked at the naked bitch next to me and smiled with fond memories of last night. My watch read 7 a.m. Who in the fuck would call now? A motherfucker better be dying to call me like this.

As I picked up the phone, I noticed that I had missed several calls from Brad. I hoped nothing happened to Candy.

"What's good?" I asked.

"It's all bad, man. You need to get here in a flash."

"What's up?"

"Just get here as soon as you can."

"I'm on my way."

I quickly dressed and went downstairs to wake up Rick. He was still knocked out with two butt-naked fine bitches on top of him. I shook him to wake him up.

"I need you to take me to the airport."

"What's going on?"

"I need to get to the city. Something bad had happened."

"Man, what's going on?"

"I don't know, but my man said I need to get back to the city fast. I hope nothing is wrong with Candy."

"Don't think like that."

"I'm just talking."

"Maybe she's having the baby."

"It could be."

***

When I landed at the airport, Brad was waiting on me. We jumped in his gray Escalade and smashed out fast. We soon arrived at University Hospital.

"Why are we here? Is Candy having the baby?"

He had an indescribable look on his face. Tears fell from his eyes. I had never seen him cry before.

I panicked. "What's going on? Did she lose the baby?"

"Something like that."

"What you mean something like that?"

"I told the doctor I wanted to be the first to tell you."

"Tell me what? Spit it out, nigga!"

"I'm sorry, but Candy, the baby, and Price are dead."

"Dead!"

"Yes."

"What? Man, stop!"

I looked in his face knew he wasn't playing. I got out and ran into the hospital. I went to the first nurse's station I saw.

"Where's Candy Bell at?"

"Sir, who are you?"

"Her husband, Keith Washington."

"I'm sorry, sir."

"What room?"

"She is in the morgue."

They weren't going to let me see Candy, but I bribed the nurse to take me down to the morgue. I was praying that this was a nightmare and I'd wake up soon. If it was true, I couldn't forgive myself for leaving her. While I was fucking some dumb bitch in Houston, Candy was dying here.

When I entered the morgue, my knees buckled and I fell to the ground crying. My head was balled up in my hands. I crawled to the table, sobbing. Brad helped me up. I couldn't even stand.

"No, no. Fuck! No!" I fell onto the floor again. Snot and tears were streaming down my face as I saw my girl. She had gotten hit in the face. "I'm sorry…I'm sorry! I swear I'm sorry. Please God. Please God."

My heart went cold. My eyes were bloodshot red and tears still rolled down my face. "Where's Price?"

"He's over here"

I was in a cold rage! His entire body was covered. I pulled the cover back. I didn't even recognize him. He had bullets holes all over his face and body. I replaced the cover.

"Brother, they're going to pay."

We left the hospital. We pulled away in Brad's truck. "Man, what happened?"

"Price was taking her to the doctor. Bruce and his crew rolled up on them at the light on Claiborne and unloaded on them."

"You know where that nigga's mother lay her head?"

"I can find out."

"Let me know."

"You want me to handle it?"

"I'll do it. That nigga going to feel what I feel."

"Okay, I got you."

At home, everything smelled like Candy. I got in the shower and tried to make the hot water wash away what I felt. I couldn't sleep in the bed. All I could smell was her White Diamond perfume. On the couch, I finally went to sleep, thinking, what if?

***

A week later, I was at Candy's funeral . I watched as her mother and her family cried. I couldn't believe I was burying them. It should have been me. This shit was about me, not them. God had punched the clock too early on them.

I kissed the casket and dropped roses on them. I walked to her mother's side. I hugged her as we watched the caskets lower into the ground.

"If you need anything, call me," I told her mother.

I got in my white Range Rover to drive to Price's funeral. Brad, Price's girl, and the rest of his friends and family were listening to the preacher. His mother was leaning on the coffin, weeping.

I couldn't take no more. I walked to my truck.

Brad followed me. "His mother stay off Jackson in a yellow house. The nigga's been laying low."

"It okay. I'll make his ass come out."

I drove down the street thinking about Price, Candy, and my son, how I had just buried them. I pulled up Jackson Street. My mind was made up. Jesus himself couldn't make me change my mind.

I pulled the strap from underneath the seat and tucked it under my arm. I walked to the porch and knocked. When Bruce's mother opened the door, I shot her in the head and walked to my truck. I didn't even watch her fall.

CHAPTER 23
Bruce

I was in my new Jag with twenty-two-inch rims and dark tinted windows. I was at the Park Way, a small neighborhood where I be getting a lot of money. I got a few niggas working for me around here. Right now, this hoe named Cat was giving me a blow job. She was a fine black hood rat that liked to fuck niggas that have money.

I was thinking about Keith. That bitch-ass nigga thought he could get away with disrespecting me in front of my crew. I'm not the type of nigga that will tolerate that shit. I'm O.G. in this shit. He wouldn't even put me down with his plug, and after all I had done for him! That nigga put out a hit on me and my right hand man. His partner Brad killed my best friend. I couldn't let that shit slide. Somebody had to pay for that shit.

My crew shot up his girl and his right hand man Price. I heard through the street that they were dead. The next time he tried to fuck with me, he would respect me. There's only one man in the city: me. He should have listened to his mother. I killed his daddy over this same kind of shit. He tried to play me like a flunky, so I put a hit on him.

"Come on, daddy. Let's go inside."

I had been laying low at this bitch's house. Shit was too hot on the streets. I knew this nigga was looking for me.

"Okay."

As I was getting out of my car, my phone rang.

"What's good, Black?" I asked.

"Man, you need to get over to your mother's house."

"What's up?"

"Just get over here."

"I'm on my way."

"Baby, what's going on?" Cat asked.

"It's my mother." I kicked her out of the car.

When I got there, I saw a wall of lights: police, fire, and ambulance. Black rushed over to me.

"Man, what's going on?"

"It's your mother."

"What happened?"

The paramedics left her house with a stretcher. A body was covered by white. I rushed over to her, but the police held me back.

"Hold on, sir. You can't go over there."

"That's my mother."

The police let me through. I knew she had heart problems.

"Let me see her."

They pulled back the sheet. I saw a bullet had destroyed her face. My knees buckled and I screamed, "No, she didn't deserve this!"

I pulled myself together. I knew who did this. I was going to get his ass. It was war time, for real. I jumped in my car. My tires squealed as I pulled out.

***

A week later, I watched as they put my mother's casket in the ground. This nigga wanted war, then war it was. I got back in my truck, pulling off. I picked up the phone, calling a couple of killers that were on my team.

"What's up, Bruce?" Tee asked.

"I need you to kill that nigga Keith."

"What's the price?"

"$100,000."

"Say no more."

I pulled my truck over to the side of the road. I put the gun to my head as tears rolled down my face. I couldn't believe I got my mother killed. She don't have shit to do with this. That nigga was down bad. All my mother did was work her whole life to take care of me. Now she was gone because of me.

I had my hands on the trigger. As I looked at myself in the rearview mirror, I couldn't bring myself to do it. I put the gun down and called Tee back.

"What's good, my G?"

"Don't worry about it."

"You sure?"
"Yeah."
"Okay. Later."
"Later."
As I pulled off, I said to myself, "I want to see that nigga when he dies."

CHAPTER 24
Keith

I was laid up at my condo with Trish. She had been chilling with me ever since she found out about Candy and Price. I had been depressed. Sometimes I felt like doing things; some days I didn't. Sometimes I didn't even worry about my hair or shaving. When it was really bad, I didn't even take a bath.

I had been really fucked up the last few months. I wasn't getting any work. I heard through the streets that there was a drought. Niggas were selling bad coke. And Bruce had $100,000 on my head. I had killed his mother, but that made me feel even worse. I kept thinking about my own mother. Her voice said I was down bad.

I gave the house in Slidell to my sister. I couldn't stay there anymore. I was glad she was going into the military. I didn't have to worry about a nigga killing her.

Bruce had the projects back on lock. But it wasn't a problem. They couldn't really make money. Every time I heard they were there, I was spinning out on them. You can't make both money and war. I had money saved; I could afford to chill. I'd been doing this shit myself, spinning on them with AK-47 in the middle of the court in broad daylight and clearing the whole courtyard. Brad had been killing those niggas too.

Diamond called. "A few of them niggas are back in town hustling in the courtyard."

"I'm on my way." I was dressed in solid black. I grabbed the Ak-47 and loaded it.

"Baby, where are you going?" Trish asked.

"To take care of business. You know the deal."

"Baby, you need to let this go."

"Let it go?"

"There's been too much bloodshed already."

"Do you hear what you're saying? He killed my family. I'm supposed to let him get away with that?"

"I'm just saying."

"Look, either arrest me, or be here when I get back. Or you can leave. I really don't give a fuck. But this shit won't end until I kill him or he kills me.

I got in my black SS Impala and smashed out. I parked at the back of the projects. I ran to the courtyard and opened fire. They tried to run, but it was too late. I chopped their asses down like Monster did them niggas in *Boyz in the Hood.* I killed two and fucked up the other two. I heard sirens nearing as I smashed out of the projects.

I got home and showered, trying to rinse the blood off me. I thought about my actions. I had thought that I would feel better every time I killed one of his people, but I didn't. I still wanted that nigga Bruce, but he'd been hiding out. He'd have to come out sooner or later. I'd be waiting.

Rick wanted me to end the war and get back to business. Bruce and I both lost family, so we were even. He would supply both of us. He wanted Bruce and me to sit down and come to an agreement. But there can only be one king in this bitch and that's me. Rick didn't like it, but he respected my mind.

The next morning, Trish's screams woke me up. I grabbed my .45 off the nightstand. I thought some niggas was trying to break in my condo.

"What the fuck's going on?" I asked.

"Your ass is on the news."

"Say what?" I looked at the TV. I saw a picture of myself. They were saying that I killed some motherfuckers in the projects, and I needed to turn myself in. I grabbed some clothes and $50,000 in cash.

"Keith, where are you going?"

"I don't have time to fuck with you right now. I'll be in touch."

"You need to turn yourself in. I can help you."

"Help me how?"

"Let me make a few calls," she said, walking out of the room. She came back in with a distraught look on her face. "They have a witness."

"Who?" I asked.

"They wouldn't give a name, but you must turn yourself in."

"Your ass is out of your mind. I need to get out of town to think about my next move." I jumped in my truck and pulled out of the parking lot.

Trish called to me. "Baby, you need to turn yourself in."

"Hell no! Stop asking me that shit."

"Tell me where you're going, at least."

"I'll tell you when I know."

CHAPTER 25
Keith

I went to my uncle's house in Atlanta. He was my mother's real brother. He was in the game back in the day. Now, he ran a bar and a couple of salons. He had a big $1.5 million house in Buckhead. He came up to me and hugged me tight.

"What's going on, nephew? You gotten into some deep shit."

"A little. I need a place to live until I can figure this shit out.

"Stay as long as you wish. Let's go in."

Uncle Ben was a tall black man. I'm talking black like midnight. He's 6'6" and favors Shaq. He played in the NBA until he blew his knee out. He got in the game, sold some heroin, and opened his businesses.

Inside, his wife greeted me with a hug. She was a high yellow woman from Lake Charles. She had a fat ass on her, and you could tell she was fine back in the day. They'd been married twenty years and had one son who had spent the last eight years in the army.

"Hey, baby, are you in hungry? I can fix some fried chicken and red beans."

"Yes, please."

"Nephew, let me show you to your bedroom."

We went to one of his guest rooms. "I appreciate this, Uncle."

"Sorry about your girl and kid."

"Thanks "

After we finished eating, we went to the backyard. He had a pool and a gray pitbull puppy.

"Light this joint up, nephew."

We sat in chairs, smoking weed and talking.

"What exactly is going on?"

"Well, Uncle, I've got a war going on with a nigga over the projects."

"I see."

"We used to be friends. He put me in the game back in the day. I started getting my own weight and he wanted me to put him down with my plug. I wasn't going to do that, so he killed Candy, Price, and my seed."

"So he was the one?"

"Yeah. I killed his mother and some of his crew."

"So you did what you had to."

"That's how I see it too."

"Are there any witnesses to this murder?"

"Yes."

"Okay, I got you. I'm going to make some moves."

"I think you should turn yourself in and fight the charges."

"Are you sure?"

"Yes. Without any witnesses or the gun, they don't have shit. You need me to pay for a lawyer?"

"I got it."

"I still have friends in New Orleans. I'll make some calls for you."

"I appreciate it."

"I told your mother I'd look out for you and your sister before she passed."

"I know. She told us that if we ever got in trouble just to call on you."

"I ain't always been a business owner. I have a past. I know the game too. And besides, family is the only thing you have."

"Love you, Uncle."

"Love you too."

We hugged.

***

Back home in New Orleans, Trish was lying naked on my bed. I had told her I was going to turn myself in. She wanted to come by first and get some dick. She wanted to take me to jail. Down here, we got some fucked-up police. Those bitches are corrupt. Some might be on Bruce's payroll and try to kill me. But that was a worry for later.

She spread her legs as I slid my nine-inch dick in her. I put her legs on my shoulders as I thrust in and out of her wet pussy.

"Yes, daddy, give me that dick. I've missed you."

I slammed into her as she came back to back. I flipped her over in elephant position – her favorite - as I grinded my dick into her.

"Fuck, baby, I'm cumming again."

She climbed on top of me, riding me like a horse. I gripped her ass cheeks, bouncing her on my dick. She bit her bottom lip and her eyes rolled in her head as she dug her nails into my chest.

"Fuck, this pussy is good," I said, as my toes curled.

"I know how to work my pussy muscles. See how tightly I'm gripping your dick."

"I'm cumming." I felt my toes and ass tightening up.

"Me too."

She came all over my dick as I shot my hot nut all in her pussy.

CHAPTER 26
Keith

Trish was dressed in her tight blue police uniform. Her black and red hair was tied back in a ponytail. She opened the back of the police car to help me out. I was handcuffed. She mouthed "I love you" as she did so.

We walked through the double glass doors into the police station. My lawyer was waiting for me. I had called him before coming. He was a fat Jewish man who had worked for my uncle back in the day. He was among the best lawyers in the city for murder defenses.

"Keith Washington? I'm Moe Green."

"Good to see you."

"We'll get you a bond hearing tomorrow and get you out of here."

"Okay."

"Your uncle's a good friend of mine. I'll look out for you. Don't worry about anything. Especially money."

They processed me in the jail. They fingerprinted me and put a red wristband on me. In Louisiana, we don't have counties. We have parishes. In New Orleans, the bands are color-coded. Yellow is for misdemeanors; orange for serious crimes without violence, like drugs and guns; and red is for violent crimes, like murders and armed robberies. When they finished processing me, I was given an orange jump suit. They let prisoners keep their tennis shoes. They handed me a blanket, cup, and few hygiene items.

The tier was dark and quiet. A chicken wire fence separated the tier in half. As you entered, there was a sign that said "Welcome. You are entering a real jail."

A dark cloud overhangs it. There's a morgue underneath it. People say this bitch is haunted. You have to be a man in this bitch, or niggas are going to fuck you over. Niggas get raped and killed in this motherfucker. Whatever happens here follows you up the river to Angola. A rep from the streets helps. Niggas knows if they do dumb shit in here, you will kill his family when you get out.

I slammed my mattress on the cot, waking motherfuckers up.

One nigga looked at me and got up. “What’s up, Keith?” He dapped me off.

“Nothing, Buck. Chilling.”

“What are you in far?”

“Two murders in the projects. You?”

“Robberies. I’ve got to go upstate in the morning. They gave me twenty-five years.”

“Word?”

“Yeah, you know. It ain’t nothing to a stepper.” Buck was an old head who smoked rocks and often robbed people. He’d been in and out of Angola a few times. He was one of those niggas who spent most of their lives in jail with only short periods of freedom. He was slim, toothless, bald, and black as midnight. Brandy, his daughter, is one of the hoes I’m fucking. A nigga just killed one of his sons in the 17th on some beef shit. He had several other kids in the projects.

“Sorry to hear about your son.”

“Yeah. I told his ass about that beef shit, but he wouldn’t listen.”

“I’m in some of that shit right now.”

“I’ve heard. With Bruce. Be careful. He don’t play fair.”

“I know.”

“I hear you’ve been fucking my daughter. Take care of her She’s just like her trifling-ass mother.”

“I got you.”

“I’m going back to sleep. I’m back on the river in the morning. My second home. I got to get some coke and a knife. I’m going to get a boy up there too. You know how prison shit goes. I’ll have you a knife when you get there.”

“No offense, but I hope I don’t come that way.”

“I feel you.”

***

The next morning, a C.O. came onto the tier and called my name. “Keith Washington. Get ready for court.”

Buck was gone. I didn't ever hear them come get him. I saw a few niggas from my hood, and some from uptown. I hollered to them as I left.

In the hallway, they put handcuffs and shackles on me. I don't know why. It wasn't like I was going ham. The docks were right around the corner from the courthouse on Tulane and Broad.

At the docks, I saw all kinds of niggas, crackheads, and bitches that were torn up. This state shit is crazy. Niggas were sleeping on the floors and benches. They get you up at 5 a.m., but court isn't scheduled until noon, if you get to go at all. I've known people that came through here and heard their stories when they got out.

They took me to the cell and took off my shackles and handcuffs and put me in the cell. I woke up a black-ass nigga so I could sit down. I'd be fucked if I'd sit on the floor. He got up looking like he wanted some smoke. I stood looking at him, waiting to see if he would jump stupid.

"What's good, my nigga? You want this stress?" I had my fists balled up, waiting for his move.

A few niggas in other cages knew me. They told me to let the nigga make it. The docks are dirty and nasty. Paint is coming off the walls and iron balls. They serve grits and cheese for breakfast in this motherfucker. I was hungry. I grabbed a plate as I waited my turn. Soon after I finished, I was called into court.

The courtroom was freezing. I walked over to stand beside Moe Green. He was wearing a gray suit. At the next table, the prosecutor was a white lady wearing a light blue dress and some cheap white shoes. Her hair was in a bun. I was trying to decide if I should stay in jail for sixty days to see if they would pick up the charges. New Orleans law dictates that if a case isn't filed in sixty days, the charges are dismissed.

"Good morning, Mr. Washington. You are being held on two charges of homicide." The judge was a fat, white woman with short black hair. "Do you understand these charges?"

"Yes, Your Honor," I answered.

My lawyer asked, "What are we thinking about bond?"

"The people request two million dollars on each count. "

"Your Honor, it is essentially the same charge."

"Yes, Mr. Green, you are correct. Bond is set at one million dollars, cash or property. Next case."

"Bond is already posted," Moe told me.

"Before I take it, I think I should sit and see if they pick it up first."

"Are you sure?"

"Yes. Don't want to give than $1,000,000 in cash if I don't have to. But if you think they'll pick it up, I need you to get me out of this motherfucker."

"I don't think they'll pick it up."

***

For fifty days. I sat in the tier of the parish jail, making store, chilling, and getting my mind right. I needed this rest. Every time I called someone though, they kept asking when I was getting out. I had to listen to Trish's ass crying about not being able to see me. She works for the police, but she was sending a nigga naked pictures and mail. Brandy got a job in the jail and was sneaking weed and dope in here. I was waiting for Diamond to come by. I was in my pressed orange jump suit and my Jordan's. In here, you can get slippers, sheets, pajamas, towels, and tennis shoes. Diamond had been riding with me like she was my girl. She had been holding a nigga down. Brad was putting money on my books, but he wasn't fucking with the jail house shit. I couldn't blame him for that.

"Washington! Visit!" announced the chubby black C.O.

I walked out of the tank. He patted me down and took me to visitation. I walked to the booth on the end. She liked sitting there because she wore small skirts without panties to let a nigga see the fat cat.

I waited for her to enter. She was wearing a small yellow miniskirt with a matching halter top. Her red hair was cut short. Her lipstick looked perfect, and I was lost in her hazel eyes. That shit did something to me. My dick got hard instantly.

She picked up the phone. "Hey, baby. How're you doing?"

"You know me. Cooling. Waiting to see if they will file these charges."

"I checked. They haven't yet."

"That's a good thing."

"If you don't get this business done, there ain't going to be no more you and me."

"I got this. I have friends at work."

"A'ight." Make it happen."

"I will."

"How come you ain't bonded out of this shit hole yet? I know you got money."

"How do you know that?"

"Nigga, I'm a hood bitch, not a dumb bitch. I know you saved for a rainy day. You're not like most of these bum-ass niggas."

"What's the latest in the hood?"

"Nothing. Bruce drops by sometimes. He still has a couple of niggas working for him, but it ain't like how you used to have the hood jumping. I need a few dollars."

"I'll tell Brad I said give it to you."

"Okay."

"Now let a nigga see that fat pussy."

She looked down the hallway. She smiled at me and put her legs on the window, spreading them to let me see that black bald pussy. I pulled out my dick, jerking off, and I listened to her moan through the phone. I shot nut all over the glass window. We moved down a booth. She slipped some joints through the hole in the window.

"Good looking out," I said.

"You know I love you."

"I know."

The C.O. announced that visit was over. "I'll come holla at you next weekend if you're still here."

***

I called Brad and had him pick me up.

"Man, that bitch Trish told me Bruce was working for the

Feds."

"So? Fuck that nigga. We ain't serving him."

"The nigga dropped my name to the Feds."

"What the fuck? He's a bitch-ass nigga."

"He's trying to get me out of the way, for real."

"I told your dumb ass to let me kill the bitch-ass nigga."

"We're past that now. Trish is trying to find out where he's at."

"We can't fuck with the nigga. He works for the Feds. We'll certainly go to jail for killing a C.I."

"If I don't take care of the nigga, we're going to the Feds for sure."

"I'm with whatever."

"I'll deal with this shit myself."

"What? You're tripping. You can't make this personal."

"It is. But mainly I don't want you caught up in it if it goes sideways. I need you to run shit out here."

"You serious?"

"Dead serious. I got this."

"What did the plug say?"

"We straight. He's got me the next time I go to Houston."

***

Later that night, I was chilling in my cell. My door popped, so I walked out. Brandy was there working on my tier.

"Come on," she said.

I went to the mop closet in the hallway. Brandy and her homegirl were working up there. Her friend was fucking a nigga on another tier and they were taking turns watching out for each other.

Brandy pulled her pants down and bent over the sink. I slid my dick into her. I grabbed her by the shoulders, slamming my dick into her wet pussy. She moaned my name out. The pussy you sneak is the best pussy. I ain't lying.

"Fuck, I'm cumming!" I shot my nut all in her.

She pulled her pants up and kissed me. "Here's the ounce of weed you wanted."

"Good looking out."

"Nigga, when are you coming home? I'm ready to quit this shit."

"Just a few more days."

"Shit, you need a hurry up, nigga. I need to get some money. The hood has dried out. Bruce has that bullshit coke in the hood, and crackheads are going other places. And there's a drought in the city."

"I'll see what I can do about it."

"Love you. Bye."

Back in my cell, I was thinking. I needed to get back out there, especially if there was a drought in the city. If these bitches didn't holler for me this week, I'd call my lawyer to come get me out this bitch. It seemed like the streets was missing a nigga.

***

It was Friday a night. I'd been here for fifty-seven days. I wanted to call my lawyer to tell him to get me out. I was tired of this shit now. I had to beat a couple of niggas up over talking some crazy shit to me about my money. They said they wouldn't pay me. I caught one of the niggas in the shower and hit him in the head with a lock. I made his ass check out the tier. The other nigga, I ran up on him with a shank and hit him in the side a couple times. A nigga ain't going to jack me in the streets. I damn sure wasn't going to let a niggas jack me over $200. I don't play. I'm a real nigga, either in here or on the streets.

Just then, they called my name. I left all my stuff to one of my homeboys out of the projects. I walked downstairs to central lock up. They had dropped the charges. The witnesses didn't want to testify. I was waiting for them to let me out. I was in the holding tank with a couple of other niggas that was getting out. I was so glad they dropped the charges. I was ready to get the fuck out of jail. I was ready to lay in my own bed. I promised I would never see the inside of a jail no more.

"Washington," a slim chick called my name.

"That's me." I walked out of the holding tank.

She looked good. She was slim with long purple hair and red lips. She was wearing a tight green uniform that held her nice ass in place. She knew I had a rep on the streets.

"What's good? When do you get off?" I asked.

"Naw, Keith. You fucking with too many hoes out there."

"What's that got to do with anything? I've got room."

"That's how you're coming?"

"You already know. What's you name."

"Rena."

"Put your number in my phone. I'll take you out of town sometime."

"Okay. Here."

"I'll give you a call."

"You better."

***

As I left central lock, Moe Green was waiting in his white 500 SL Benz. I jumped in and he pulled off.

"Man, thank you for everything."

"Not a problem. If you need me for anything else, let me know."

"Hey, I want you to be my personal lawyer. Do you do drug cases?"

"I fight them too. But I have a good friend of mine named Baldwin. He's good with that type of stuff. I'll tell him about you."

"Good. Get with me tomorrow."

"Okay."

***

I got out of the shower. It was midnight. I heard the doorbell ring. Trish was there in a red Uniqlo dress with a big smile on her face.

"Can I come in?"

"Yes."

She came in and took off her dress and let it fall to the floor. She was naked beneath it. I picked her up and carried her to the bedroom, where I fucked the shit out of her.

CHAPTER 27
Keith
Fall 1999

After I got out, I traded in all my cars to cop a black Bentley with the wood grain steering wheel, black leather seats, and twenty-eight-inch chrome rims. It had hit me for $250,000. I admit I was tripping, but I needed to floss up a little. The little niggas needed to know that I hadn't fallen off, that I still got it.

I wasn't selling work yet. I was chilling. My people were mad at me. They were ready to eat. There was a drought in the city. Coke prices were high, and niggas only had bad coke. I had Diamond and Trish trying to find a line on that nigga Bruce. Rick was hitting me up to try to talk me into coming down to Houston and to get back in the game.

I rode Super Sunday around the Magnolia to check out the bad bitches and look at niggas flossing, I had them niggas' heads turning when they saw my big boy Bentley. I carried my gun on my lap. I had to be cautious and watch everything. I wasn't planning on parking; I was just riding through.

My phone rang. I didn't recognize the number. "What's good? Who's this?"

"Rena."

"Who?"

"We met when you were getting out of central lockup "

"Oh yeah, I remember now."

"You said you wanted a hoe to call you."

"I'd forgotten. It took you a long time to call."

"Yeah, things have been busy."

"I hear you. That nigga must have let you out to play."

"Boy, ain't no nigga going to tell me what to do. I don't even have a nigga or a baby daddy."

"Oh yeah?"

"Nigga, you probably got a few kids running around the city with ten baby mommas."

"No. Not really."

"Why? Is it because you don't claim them?"
"It's because I don't have any."
"Where you at?"
"Riding around the city."
"I thought we were supposed to go out? That's what you told me."
"I know."
"So what's good? Were you lying?"
"The one thing I don't do is lie. You ever been to Florida?"
"No."
"You want to go?"
"When are we going?"
"Today, if possible. Where you stay?"
"Off Freret and Napoleon in the 13th. Behind the hospital."
"We can make that happen."
"Look, my friend wants to come."
"She must be fucking. This ain't free ride."
"Damn, like that?"
"Straight like that. What did you think? This shit was free? She needs to be down with getting fucked."
"Boy, whatever. Can she come or not?"
"You heard what I said?"
"It's all good."
"I'll holla at you later."
"Don't be playing. "
I got you."
After I hung up, Brad called me.
"Man, what are we doing?"
"What are you talking about?"
"Meet me at Jena."
"I'll meet you in thirty."

***

Brad was waiting on the sidewalk when I got there.
"What's good, my nigga?" I dapped him off.

"Man, a nigga needs to make some moves to eat."

"I told you we were going to chill for a minute."

"It's good for you. You've got some money saved. But a nigga like me needs to eat."

"I feel you."

"What are you going to do?"

"I'll holla at the plug and see what's up. When I get back, I need to handle some business."

"I need some hold over money."

"You want to come with me to Florida?"

"Naw, nigga. My money ain't right."

"I got you. I have a bad bitch that is bringing a friend with her."

No, nigga, you know how I roll. I need my own bread. I ain't into that shit."

"I'll get the hoe Diamond to shoot you something to hold you over."

"Nigga, you got shit? You're just sitting on it?"

"We going to be straight. Don't trip."

"You know that Dave is getting out in a few minutes."

"Yeah, we're straight. I got him."

"A'ight. It's all on you."

In Jena, I ordered a hot sausage po'boy. As I ate, I thought about what Brad said. I couldn't just lay up. I had to get back in the game. My people had to eat. They were looking to me to make money. I went to a self-storage building in Slidell. I kept twenty bricks and $2 million in a large safe. I took out three bricks and put them in my LV bag. I called Brad and told him to meet at my condo. When I got back, he was waiting for me in his red Range Rover.

I got in and handed him the bag. "Here, my nigga. That's three bricks. I'll get with you when I get back. Love you."

CHAPTER 28
Keith

Rena, Tina, and I walked out of the airport in Miami. Tina was a sexy redbone. The ladies were wearing matching white and pink leggings and halters. We got into a black SUV that I had rented.

"Bitch, I can't believe we're here," Tina said.

"Bitch, I told you he wasn't faking. Light that blunt up."

This was my first trip too. I had always wanted to come here. I had heard about all the bad bitches and boss niggas and how South Beach was so live. All the rap niggas talked about how live it was here. From all the foreign cars, it looked as if they weren't lying. I saw Ferraris, Roll Royces and Lamborghinis, just to name a few. Shit, you buy that in my city, the Feds will come knocking at your door. Well, you can buy it, but you can't be flossing in it every day like they do here. It's common to see it down here. Shit, this is where coke first came in.

We were staying at Hilton on South Beach. We had a suite on the seventh floor at $1000 a night. My plan was to relax, hit the clubs, and fuck these hoes. The suite was huge. There were two bedrooms and a living room laid out with white couches. The bathroom had a huge tub. As they got dressed, I saw them pop some pills. It looked like X. This was the newest fad. Hoes get real freaky on that shit. I'd never tired it.

"What's good?" I said.

"You want to pop one?" Rena asked.

"I ain't never fucked with that shit before."

"It won't do shit to you except keep your dick hard. You'll need it to keep up with us. When we take it, we want to fuck all night." Tina popped a blue pill after speaking.

I decided to go for it. I popped my first X.

We hit a club called The Mansion. They had bad bitches of all nationalities. It made me wish I never brought these hoes with me. They were all dressed skimpy with their asses hanging out. I tipped the bouncer to get in the VIP. I ordered bottles of Patron and Ace of Spades. We stayed there getting fucked up until the club closed.

***

Back at the hotel, Rena and Tina stripped. I watched as they ate each other out. My dick was hard as concrete. I joined them. They took turns sucking my dick and licking my balls as I ate them out. I fucked them both from the back as they tongue kissed each other. We fucked until I couldn't anymore. I busted a couple nuts and them hoes swallowed every drop.

As I passed out, they continued with each other.

I awoke the next morning and saw both of them passed out. We stayed in Miami a week. I spent my time fucking different hoes with and without Rena and Tina. We had four and five-somes. I met a lot of rappers and had pictures taken with them. Shit was live in Miami. I didn't want to leave. When my money got super right, I was coming back. This was going to be my new city.

CHAPTER 29
Keith
2000

It was a new year. The 2000's were rolling in. B.G.'s song "Bling Bling" was still booming. DMX was still hot. Murder Inc. with Ja Rule started tearing up the rap industry. I was now getting 1000 keys a month. Tina, Rena, Brandy, and Diamond were making frequent tips to Houston in trucks built to hide at least a hundred keys. I was paying thirteen apiece for them. My whole crew was eating.

I had brought a warehouse in Kenner where I stashed the keys. There were still a few other niggas getting work, but I had the cheapest prices in the city. I had a mission: to become the King of New Orleans. I knew there would be beef, but I didn't care. I was going to take over all the projects and supply the whole city. I wanted to gain control of a few other states. You'd either get it from my team, or your ass wouldn't eat.

I was waiting on my drivers at the warehouse. Ten minutes later, they were pulling their trucks into the warehouse. I had workers to take the truck apart and pull coke from them. Brad was in charge of guns and enforcement. Once Dave got out tomorrow, he would be in charge of collecting payments from people who think they didn't have to pay.

"How did the trip go?"

"It was good," Diamond answered.

She was in charge of the pick-up and dropping keys to the people I fronted work to. I paid them twenty stacks. They all knew I was fucking all of them, but they weren't tripping. They wanted to get this bread. I tried to keep the dick out of them. Business and pussy didn't mix. I still fucked both Diamond and Trish.

Trish's partner worked for me to move work and money around the city. Trish's partner was a slim, blonde white chic. I was paying them fifty grand for each move, a lot more than the police paid them. I even had customers across the river in Jefferson Parish. Those motherfuckers are racist over there. If they caught a nigga over there, they'd give him life.

I let the white chick drop off the dope. A couple niggas over there got between 100 to 200 bricks.

"Hey, baby." Trish kissed me.

"Hey."

"Okay, is everything ready?" Trish asked

"Yeah. Put the bags in y'all police cars now."

"Okay." He put a hundred keys in four bags into their cars and gave them $50,000 apiece.

"I'm coming over tonight," Trish said.

"We must be going to fuck him together," Diamond said.

"I ain't tripping."

They got in their cars and left.

"Diamond, drop twenty keys off to Tootie in the projects.

"I don't know why you fuck that stink hoe anyway."

"Look, I don't have time for bullshit. Handle business."

"You make me sick."

CHAPTER 30

Keith

Brad and I were picking up Dave in my new black Rolls that hit me for $350,000. I heard through the streets that Bruce had been arrested by the Feds on coke and gun charges. I also heard he had been shooting heroin. He had been laying low. I was kind of looking for him. If I caught him, I'd kill him. But I was more focused on getting this money than him.

"So what's that nigga Lester talking about in the Magnolia? Is he going to get down or is he talking that war shit?" I asked Brad.

"He's talking about that war shit."

"How about Wayne in the Melpomene?"

"He's COO."

"Duck in the St. Thomas?"

"You know he ain't going for it. These niggas really think they are on top."

"They can't ever be. I'll move in on them and my coke cheaper. We'll take care of that in a bit. Rick said that he needs to talk to me."

We got to the Hunt's Correctional Center. It was white and different dorms were around it. Inmates were working both inside and outside the prison. Lots of inmates were lifting weights on the yard.

"Man, this nigga going to be as big as shit. You know the nigga going to get put down as soon as he touches the city."

"I know. That's why I got shit put on the side for his ass. I wish Price was here to see us."

"He's watching us. He's got our back."

"Don't tell the nigga about the surprise."

"What?"

The trip to Vegas."

"Yeah. I got you."

We stood outside the car waiting for him. At eight, he came out in the Polo gear I had sent him. We hugged him tightly.

"My nigga, you free."

"I ain't got shit."

"Nigga, you know I got you."

"You'd better."

"Nigga, you big as a motherfucker. Those hoes will love you out here," Brad said.

"Yes, nigga, this what happens when you do fifteen years in prison."

"I feel you."

"Come on, let's bounce," I said.

We jumped in my whip and pulled off.

"Nigga, this how you're coming?"

"You already know," I replied. "Brad has one too."

"Mine red though."

"Niggas, I want one all-white."

"It's all good."

***

Once we landed in Vegas, I immediately took Dave shopping. I spent thirty grand on him. I got us the President's suite. When we got into the room, I had two bad butt-naked strippers waiting to serve Dave up.

"Niggas, that's what I'm talking about. I love you niggas."

He took the hoes into the bedroom with him. Brad and I dealt with the rest over the night. It was a big orgy in the motherfucker. We had twenty bad bitches and threw a party. We stayed in Vegas for three weeks partying and living it up.

"I had a good time in Vegas."

"That's what's up."

When we got back to New Orleans, Brad went to check on shit. I took Dave to a dealership where I had a hook up. I had a nigga hooking me up with cars and fixing it where it looked like I owned a business so the Feds couldn't get me.

"My nigga, I want a white one."

"Okay, Larry, hook him up."

"I got him."

I handed Larry $300,000 in a bag, and Dave left in a brand new Rolls. I bought him a condo in Slidell, and gave him $100,000.

"Nigga, this all yours."

"Man, I appreciate you looking out."

"I told you I got you."

"I know. Look, I need some of them keys to get my money right."

"My nigga, slow down. Enjoy your freedom."

"You know how it is. A nigga wants his own money."

"Don't trip. I need to go out of town. When I get back, we'll talk."

"I'm sorry about what happened to your girl and baby."

"Me too."

"I'm sorry Price can't be here."

"Me too."

"What's up with Bruce?"

"Last I heard, the nigga got knocked by the Feds."

"You think he'll talk?"

"I don't care. I wasn't fucking with him anyway."

"If you need me to put in work, I'm up for it."

"I know. Appreciate it."

"Look, I got to bounce. I'll fuck with you when I get back."

"Thanks for the love. I don't know where I would be if it wasn't for you, because a nigga didn't have shit getting out."

"It's all love."

CHAPTER 31
Bruce

I was in an interrogation room looking at the black one-way mirror. This was supposed to be state shit. I should have been able to bond out. All that happened was the NOPD busting a nigga with some guns and keys of heroin. A nigga was getting loaded, I admit. That bitch-ass nigga Keith had a lock on coke in the city. He was trying to take over everything. He had a strong team behind him. I couldn't catch him alone. I was curious as to why the Feds wanted me. I took a drag on my cigarette.

Two white guys carrying folders and wearing black suits came in. They sat across from me.

"Bruce Black? I'm Agent White. This is Agent Bennett."

"What do y'all want with me? I just got busted with some dope and guns."

"That's why we're here. You have a prior felony conviction. It's illegal for you to possess a firearm."

"That's not federal."

"There's been a lot of killing in the city. The Feds are coming in to fix it."

"Man are you serious? The Feds are stooping to the state level to file charges now?"

"Mr. Bennett is with the ATF."

"What do you want from me?"

"Do you know this man?" He put a picture of Keith in front of me.

I could tell them no. But if they got him out of the way, I could take over again. Beside, this fucking nigga killed my eighty-year-old mother. "Why do you want to know?"

"We believe he is a major supplier of cocaine in New Orleans. We're trying to get close to him."

"I'm listening."

"We need you to try to get in with him."

"I can't do that. He thinks I killed some of his people."

"Find out something. And report to us."

"You want me to be a rat?"

"You do us this favor, and we'll do you one. We can make your charges go away. Or you can get thirty years in federal prison. We will make sure the charges stick. Take your time to think about it."

They left. I was fucked either way. With my jacket, they'd hang me. The first rule I told Keith was never to tell on friends. But he ain't my friend. Fuck him.

They came back in about thirty minutes.

"What's it going to be?"

"I'll do it."

"Welcome aboard."

CHAPTER 32
Keith

When I got back to the city, Trish called and said she needed to see me immediately.

I got to Copeland's on St. Charles.

She was waiting on me in the restaurant in her uniform. She kissed me, and we sat down.

"Your name was dropped to the Feds," she said.

"What?"

"It's true. It just came cross my captain's desk."

"Do you know who did it?"

"Bruce."

"I know he got busted by NOPD with heroin and guns."

"But the Feds came in. The department is cooperating."

"Damn. Where is that nigga at now?"

"He's out. Working."

"I need to get this nigga."

"Didn't you hear me say he was working for the Feds?"

"If I don't kill him, they'll have my ass in the Feds."

"What you need me to do?"

"Find out where his ass at. And let me know."

"I got you. I'm coming over tonight."

CHAPTER 33
Keith
Two months later

I was riding around with that nigga Bruce in my truck wrapped in duct tape. He had been hiding in a motel on Airline Highway. He had reneged on the Feds and was hiding from them and getting high. Trish told me that they got a tip that he was there. I busted into his hotel room and put him in the trunk.

As I pulled away from the parking lot, I saw police cars pulling in. I really didn't know what I was going to do with Bruce. Then it came to me.

I stayed on Airline until I got to an old abandoned hotel with an alligator pond behind it. A lot of O.G. niggas used to bring bodies there to get rid of them."

I thought about my decision to kill him. He did give me the game and taught me the rules to the game. But then he broke all of them. Also, he killed Candy, Price, and m unborn child, something I would never forgive him for."

Tears rolled down my face. I got out of the car with my gun in my hand. I opened the trunk and ripped the tape of his mouth.

"Nigga, you got any last words?"

"This how you're going to do me? After all I taught you, and all I did for you?"

"Nigga, you taught me a lot and gave me the rules of the games. But the most important rules was, never tell on friends."

"I didn't go through with it."

"You killed my wife and kid."

"You killed my mother."

"I did. There can only be one king in the city."

"I'll go away. You won't have to worry about me again."

"I know."

I shot him in the head twice. I dragged him to the pond and threw him in. I watched as the alligators obliterated his body. I thought it would make me feel better, but it didn't.

I went to the cemetery on Airline to the graves of Candy and

Price. I knelt in front of their graves, my eyes full of tears-

"I miss y'all so much. I'd give anything to get y'all back. I love and miss you. I killed that nigga who killed you. So rest in peace. Price, I miss you, bro. I'm about to take over the city like you said I would. I'm doing it for us. You will always be in my heart. I love you."

CHAPTER 34
Keith

"Suck that dick."

I held a handful of her hair as Brandy deep-throated my dick. She sucked and licked the swollen head of my dick. I was about to cum. She went faster, choking and slobbing on it. I busted a nut in her mouth as she swallowed my load.

She didn't stop. She got it back hard. I bent her over the dresser and slammed my dick in and out of her wet pussy as I finger fucked her asshole. She bit her bottom lip as she watched me in the mirror.

"Fuck, daddy. Don't stop. I'm about to cum."

"Shit, this pussy is fire."

As I was about to cum, my door burst open. I started to reach for my gun, but I saw it was the police. I raised my hands as they rushed to serve me. They let us get dressed. They left her there.

I was taken to the 7th district station in Eastern New Orleans. I was put in an interrogation room. Shortly, Trish came in.

"What the fuck is going on?" I asked.

"They're trying to get you for murder."

"Whose murder?"

"Bruce."

Two black federal agents in black suits came in the room. Trish left. "I need a lawyer."

"For what? You do something?" the first agent said.

"I'm Agent Frost, this is Agent Black. We just need to ask you some questions."

"I need you to call my lawyer and talk to him."

"We just need to ask you some questions about Bruce."

"Who?"

They showed me a picture of him.

"I said I need my lawyer."

I heard a knock on the window. Baldwin, the lawyer I hired after Moe Green retired, was considered the best in the city. I paid him $20,000 a month for shit like this.

"If you're not arresting my client, we're leaving. Grab your things."

I looked at them and walked out.

"We'll see you soon," Agent Black said.

I wasn't worried about them ever finding Bruce. He was sleeping with the gators and nobody knew about it but me.

CHAPTER 35
Keith

I was in Bunker Hill, one of the hoods in the eastern part of New Orleans. I pushed a lot of coke here. I was shooting dice with Dave and Ro and a few other niggas who I fronted keys to around in the East. We were outside Jackie's house. Jackie was a brown-skinned, big-ass stripper hood bitch who did hair on the side. Dave had been fucking her since he'd been home.

I saw a red BMW pull up in front her house. I had never seen it before. A redbone stepped out wearing tight pink shorts, a pink halter top, and white and pink Air Max's. Her wavy black hair hung long in a wet look. I smiled at her. She was thick with a nice-sized ass. I had to talk to her. I couldn't let her pass. Shorty looked damn fine.

"Excuse me, beautiful. I'm Keith. How are you doing?"

"Fine," she replied with an attitude.

"Damn, baby girl. I'm just trying to holla. I've never seen you here before."

"You've never seen me because I'm not from around here."

"Red, you don't have to get an attitude with a brother. I just found you attractive. I wanted to take you out and get to know you better."

She stared me down before finally cracking a smile. "You're kind of cute. How do you know I don't already have a man?"

"I'm not worrying about that. If you go out with me, you'll never go back to him."

"Is that right?"

"It's a fact."

"Arrogant, aren't we?"

"Not at all. I just go for what I want. And right now, I'm trying to win over a beautiful woman's heart."

"I bet you say that to every woman you trying to date."

"Is it working?"

"A little bit."

"Can you give me your number so I can call you?"

"No."

"Like that?"

"I'll take your number though."

"Here you go. Put it in your phone, and make sure you call me."

"I'm Shantell." She smiled and stretched out her hand.

"Keith." I kissed her hand.

"Nice to meet you."

"Same here, and have a blessed day."

I watched her fine ass go up the stairs and knock on Jackie's door. She looked back and smiled when she caught me looking at her ass.

***

Shantell

I went into Jackie's house. I was still smiling as I picked up a blunt.

Jackie sat down next to me. "What's your ass all cheesed up about?" She took the blunt from me and hit it.

"A fine brother was shooting dice in your driveway. He stopped me and gave me his number."

"Which one? Who?"

"He said his name was Keith."

"Be careful with his ass. He's a major drug dealer in the game, And he's a player. He has a thousand hoes on his dick. I've heard the nigga is hung like a house. Those hoes' hair I fix come in here and run their mouths. I'm fucking his homeboy Dave. He just got out of prison. You know I like that prison dick."

"It's not like I'm going to marry him or anything. He just wants to take me out."

"Don't say I didn't warn you. Don't come crying to me when he drops that dick in you and break your heart and has your ass dick whipped."

"Who says I'm fucking him?"

"It's not if; it's when."

"Whatever, bitch. You ready to go get beauty supplies?"

"Yes"

"How long are you going to be home?"

"Just until spring break is over"

"Let me grab my purse."

When I walked out, they were still shooting dice. I smiled at him, and he showed me his pearly white teeth back. I got a good look at the brother. He was fine as hell.

CHAPTER 36
Keith

I was shaking the dice as my phone rang. "What's good?" I said.

"Man, I need 200 of those things."

"We'll meet at the same spot in an hour." I hung up. "Come on, Dave. Let's roll."

Dave was my wingman, my second right hand. Brad liked doing his own thing; he really just liked fucking around with us when it was time to kill motherfucker or to go collect from a motherfucker I fronted work to. Otherwise, he was at his house chilling with a few bitches.

We got in the car. "Who was that?" Dave asked.

"Larry."

"What he wanted?"

"200."

"What are we going to do about that nigga who ran in the dope house and got the workers out of twenty-five bricks?"

"Chill, I got a line on him."

"That's what I'm talking about. We can't let any of these fuck niggas make it out here. What's good on the plug? I thought we were making major moves out here."

"Be cool. I got this."

We go to the warehouse. There were 200 keys on the table. I don't serve people usually, but Larry wouldn't fuck with nobody but me. I'd been serving him for a long time.

He came in with his right hand man. Larry was black as midnight with a bald head. He was as tall as a basketball player and looked like Michael Jordan. He was from Baton Rouge, another part of Louisiana, an hour away. He ran things up there and got 200 bricks every time he came down.

"What's good, Larry?"

"You got me."

"You already know. Where the money?"

His right hand man got the bags out of the truck. He came back with two brown leather bags and put them on the table. I ran the money through a counting machine. It took almost an hour to count four million dollars. I had the bricks loaded in a car and truck stash spots.

"Good looking out, Keith." He dapped me off and left.

I had them coming from all parts of Louisiana and Mississippi, but I needed more product. I had to associate with a cartel to get to the next level.

Brad called. "I got the nigga."

"Where're you at?"

"Warehouse two."

"We're on the way." I hung up. "Come on, Dave. We need to go."

***

At the other warehouse, Brad and a couple of his workers had this nigga named Boo tied up. This warehouse was where I brought niggas, undercover police officers, and rats to kill them. There's gator's in the river out back.

Boo had hit one of my spots, killed two workers, and took twenty-five bricks. Normally in this situation, if you hit one of my shops, I would find you and put you to work to work off the debt, but since he killed my workers, I couldn't let that slide. Boo was from the St. Thomas projects. A lot of those niggas back there, all they do is rob big-time drug dealers.

I dapped Brad off. "Good looking out."

Boo was short, chubby, and brown-skinned. He had dreads and tattoos everywhere. He had a graveyard under his belt. I looked into his bloody face,

"Nigga, did you really think you could jack me and get away with it?"

"Nigga, fuck you. I ain't scared of you."

"You should be." I pulled out my gun and shot him in the head. "Feed his ass to the gators."

"You got it, boss." Brad and Dave took him away.

CHAPTER 37
Shantell

I was reading one of my business textbooks for school. My grades had been slipping from messing with Brittney's ass. I had been slipping a lot. My mother didn't even know.

I didn't live on campus anymore. I had moved to an apartment with Brittney. We'd taken several trips to different parts of Louisiana. She paid me well. I had a new BMW. I had told my mother that it was Brittney's car.

She had met Brittney. She came to New Orleans with me during spring break and she had spent part of this summer here. She asked if we were a couple when she caught us sleeping in the bed together. I lied and told her that we were just close. It was true. We had slept together, but we were not a couple. She even had a boyfriend. I was her side piece. The bitch was taking care of me. I always had the latest everything. Besides, while all that licking was good, I needed a man. I needed me some dick badly.

I thought about Keith. He was fine. I hope he remembered me, because it'd been a couple months since the day we met. I had gone back to college, so I never got around to calling him.

His phone rang twice.

"Hello?" he answered.

His raspy voice sent chills up my spine. My pussy got soaking wet.

"This is Shantell."

"Who?"

It seemed like he had forgotten me. "Damn. Do you have that many hoes calling you?"

"It's not like that. I'm just a busy guy."

"I can call you when you have more time."

"I'm sorry. I was joking. I know who you are. You're the fine pretty woman I met at Jackie's house."

"That's me."

"I was expecting to hear from you earlier. It's been a minute."

"Sorry. I've been busy too."

"It's cool. Can I take you out sometime?"

"What about tonight?"

"Yes. I can do tonight," he said.

"I'll get ready." I gave him my address.

"I'll pick you up at eight."

I got in the shower. When I finished, my bedroom clock said seven-thirty. I put on some peach Victoria's Secret lotion. I was wearing a white Victoria's Secret thong and bra. I topped it off with my white Chanel dress with a pair of white wedge heels.

By the time I finished, it was time. I sprayed on some Chanel perfume. I heard the doorbell. I grabbed my purse and ran down the stairs. I needed to get to the door before my mother did. Her ass was very judgmental when it came to the men I dated.

I was too late. She was opening the door when I came downstairs.

Keith was so handsome. He was wearing a black suit and Gucci loafers. He had a handful of red and white roses.

"Can I help you?" my mother asked.

"Yes, ma'am. I'm here to pick up Shantell for a date."

I got in front of her to stop her from asking a thousand questions. "Come on. Let's go. I love the flowers." I handed them to my mother. "I'll be out late, so don't wait up."

We left. As we got into his car, he opened the door for me like a gentleman. If he kept this up, he might get some pussy tonight.

He took me to a restaurant called Houston's in Slidell.

"May I take your order?" a waitress asked.

I started to answer, but he broke in. "May I?" he asked.

"Sure."

"Give us the lobster tail, grilled shrimp, and baked potatoes with everything. And bring us a bottle of red wine."

"Coming up, sir."

"Tell me a little about yourself," he asked me.

"I was born in the Melpomene Projects, but I was raised in the eastern part of New Orleans by my mother and stepdaddy. I'm going to the University of Houston right now."

"What are you majoring in?"

"Business."

"Pretty and smart. That's a great combination."

"Thanks. Tell me about you?"

"What you heard? I know Jackie told you something."

"She did, but I want to hear it from you."

"I'm a hustler."

"You sell drugs?"

"I do."

"When are you planning on giving the streets up? I can't marry a guy and have kids for him if he's going to jail or ends up dead in the streets."

"Wait. Hold up. Married? Kids? This a little fast, don't you think? This is our first date."

"If you think you're just going to hit this ass and be gone in the morning, we can end this shit now."

"Damn, you're straightforward."

"I'm not stupid or a little girl. I'm twenty-five and from New Orleans. You're a drug dealer. And I've dated a few. All you guys are out for one thing: ass."

"That's the biggest problem with women. They all think drug dealers are alike. But we all are different."

"You don't chase hoes to fuck them? Tell me I'm lying."

"Actually, women chase me to fuck me."

"Who are you supposed to be?"

"A man who knows how to treat women in the bedroom."

"Oh, really? Here's how I see it. I like you. Do you like me?"

"Most definitely. Without a doubt."

"Okay, then let's go."

"We just got here."

"I'm ready."

"What did I do wrong?"

***

As soon as we got to his condo, we started taking off one another's clothes. He ripped my thong off, picked me up, and pinned me against the wall. He shoved every bit of his nine inch, big hard dick up in my tight soaking wet pussy, filling my pussy walls. I dug my nails into his back as he went even deeper in me. I felt him all in my stomach.

He thrust his cock in my cumming wet pussy until I came all over his dick back to back. He put me down and bent me over the couch. I spread my ass cheeks as he slammed his dick in my pussy. I gripped his black leather sofa, ripping a hole in it. It was pleasure and pain at the same time, but I didn't want him to stop.

"I'm cumming!" I yelled, shaking.

"Me too."

He gripped my ass cheeks and pushed even deeper in my pussy as he shot his hot nut in me. I came back to back on his dick.

We went into his bedroom where we fell asleep with my head on his chest.

The next morning he wasn't in the bed with me. I got up and walked around calling out his name. I went to the bathroom to take a much-needed piss after that nigga beat my pussy up. The brother know how to put it down and he was hung like a horse.

I put on a Saints T-shirt and went to the living room. I found a letter and some flowers. I read the letter. It said: "I'm sorry I had to run. Something came up. Stay as long as you want. I left you a key to the condo on the table along with $1000. Buy yourself something nice. I hope to see you when I get back. I had a great time last night."

I sat back on the sofa and smiled as I smelled the flowers.

***

That evening, I went over to see Jackie with a pleased pussy and a big smile. I was talking to Jackie's hating ass while we smoked a blunt.

"I take it you and Keith are more than friends?" she said.

"What makes you say that?"

"Let's see. The big-ass smile on your face. The glow you got going on. And you're walking funny. So were the rumors about his dick size true?"

"They're true. Bitch, the nigga is hung like a donkey."

We laughed and slapped five.

"He knows how to use it?"

"Had a bitch climbing a wall - literally. The nigga had me in the air bouncing me off his dick. I thought he was going to bust through me. I came so much, it was a shame. I see why those hoes chase him."

"I told you that. When will you see him again?"

"He had some business to go to out of town. It'll be a few days."

"I'm telling you, this nigga has bitches. Don't get your heart wrapped up in this nigga, or your shit is going to be broken."

"I can take it. I got this."

"You know how many hoes that come through my shop saying this? The next few days those hoes are sick that he dropped their ass and is fucking the hoe sitting next to them. I've seen so many fights over the nigga that it's a shame."

"I'm not a weak bitch like those hoes. I'm not getting into a street fight over some nigga. He'll be running behind me before I'm running after him. I promise you that."

"I hear you, but that hoe between your legs is going to be saying something else when your ass is running around here dick whipped."

"I don't get dick whipped. I whip the dick. Remember that."

"I will."

CHAPTER 38
Keith

I walked up to Rick's front door. He kept telling me that I needed to meet an important person. I had been telling him I want to be king of my city. He told me this guy could put me there.

Rick answered the door. "I'm glad you made it."

"You said you could introduce me to someone who could take me to the next level of the game."

"This is true. Let's have a drink while we're waiting on him."

We went to his living room and were talking over glasses of wine.

"How's everything on your end?" Rick asked.

"Good."

"I'm glad you killed the beef shit."

"Me too," I lied. "War and money don't mix - unless you're the cartel.

"What do you know about the cartels?"

"I know they're tied to the Columbians cartels. The cartels flood the United States with cocaine."

"You're right."

"What are you getting at?"

"You have to trust me."

Two men snuck up behind me, putting a black hood on my head.

"Rick, man, what the fuck is this?" I struggled to get away.

"If you want to meet the big dog and get to the next level, this is how it has to happen. He wants to meet you."

I stopped struggling and let them lead me to a car. I wondered if this was how the cartel did shit, or if maybe Rick messed with their money and blamed it on me so they were going to kill my ass. If I made it out of this, I was going to kill Rick's ass for playing me like this. He could have given me a heads up. He supposed to be my boy.

In a few hours, the car stopped. I was helped from the car and the hood was pulled from my head. My eyes blinked and watered as they adjusted to the sun and dust. I soon saw a short Mexican man wearing black cowboy boots. In fact, he was entirely dressed like a cowboy with black jeans and a western shirt and a brown cowboy hat. He had a mustache and smoked a cigar. I was wondering who this motherfucker was. I had never seen him in my life. I also didn't know why I was in the middle of a fucking desert.

"Do you know who I am?" he asked.

"No. Am I supposed to know you?"

"You should. You move a lot of my product through your city. Come with me."

As I followed him to his black Benz, it hit me. This was the boss of the motherfucking cartel.

As his driver pulled off, he said, "Tell me about yourself."

"I'm Keith Washington out of New Orleans from the Calliope projects. Apparently, I've come from selling nickel rocks to meeting the head of a cartel."

"So now you know who I am?"

"Not exactly. But the only person you might go to meet with in the middle of a desert who has a thousand bodyguards has to be a boss."

"Correct. My name is Deloso. I'm the boss of the cartels along the Southern border. Nothing moves unless I order it. The Zeta's Cartel work for me and does all my dirty work."

"I'm feeling that."

"'Tell me about your family?"

"My mother is dead. My father was killed in the projects. It's just me and my sister."

"Any kids?"

"No." I saw no need to tell him I had one killed during a war. It might make him not want to fuck with a nigga. I needed this plug.

"You need to make some. You make a lot of money. Failing to spend is no fun."

"I hear you."

"Have you ever been to jail?"

"Yes, both as a juvenile and an adult."

"For what?"

"Drugs and murder."

"What do you think about a rat?"

"I think they're the lowest motherfuckers on earth."

"Glad to hear it. I need you to handle something for me."

"Anything."

When we arrived at his ranch, a bodyguard opened the door for him. He must have owned 500 acres. Black and white horses ran around everywhere. His house was made of white brick, and it was huge. A large white stone fence ran around the property. It was like something from the movie *Scarface*. Workers were running everywhere like ants.

Inside the house, a Mexican maid greeted me. "Would you like something to drink?"

"Yes, thank you."

I followed him through several rooms. There was marble and wood everywhere as well as tons of antiques. He fixed a drink and brought it to me.

We sat on a large white leather couch talking. "I hear you're moving 1000 kilos a month."

"Yes, I go pick them up in Houston."

"You must have a good team."

"I do. They're loyal to me."

"Let's go. I need to show you something."

We walked out back to a big red barn. When the door was opened, a bald black man was hanging in front of me. He was naked and bleeding. Two bodyguards were next to him. Both had guns.

"What do you think he did?"

"Something he shouldn't have."

"What do you think about him?"

"Nothing. I don't even know that motherfucker."

"You're right. He did something wrong."

"Which was?"

"Trying to infiltrate my organization. He's an undercover agent for the FBI. I found out from a source at the Bureau. I have friends everywhere. I pay off police, politicians, and even judges. You said you don't like rats?"

"Hate them."

He spoke in Spanish to one of his men. He walked over and handed me a gun. Deloso ordered, “Kill him.”

I looked at the man. He was screaming through his duct tape. It was too late to turn back. If I wanted to get to the next level, I had to demonstrate my loyalty. If I needed to, I would put a bullet in his head. But he was not a regular nigga. He was FBI. Killing a nigga on the streets is one thing. A federal agent is a different ball game. If anyone found out, my ass would get the needle. If I didn’t kill him, I’d be hanging there next.

“Fuck that shit.” I pulled the gun up and shot him in the head.

Deloso took the gun from me and shot him again. I watched the guards take the body down. “Welcome to the Gulf Coast Cartel.” He hugged me. He turned to his guards. “Bury the fucking body in the desert.”

In the other barn, there were a lot of butt-naked Mexican women. They were packing kilos of cocaine on the table.

“This is pure cocaine, straight from Columbia. I run everything in the South. Name a state and I supply it with 5000 keys a month at least.”

“There’s that much work here?”

“I get it by the tons. And Rick told me you want to be the man in your city.”

“I’m trying to take that bitch over.”

“You know that when you take over, there will be war?”

“Yes.”

“Are you ready for that?”

“Yes.”

“You’ll never have another drought.”

“That’s what I like to hear.”

“I’ll send you 2000 keys a month.”

“What price?”

“11.5 a key.”

“Do I have to come get it?”

“No. It will be delivered.”

“I’m with it.”

We shook hands.

"Good. Let's go eat."

***

A few days later, I watched as Deloso's Mexican workers unloaded a U-Haul at my warehouse. I was getting coke much cheaper, and I didn't have to go get it. If I needed more, it was all love. They were even fronting me these motherfuckers. That's what's good about fucking with a real plug. You never have to worry about a drought.

"Nigga, it's on now," Dave said.

"Yeah, we can take over some shit."

Dave said, "This shit ain't going to be easy. A lot of bloodshed comes with it. Are y'all ready for war?"

"Hell, yeah," everyone answered as one.

"Then it's on. Let's take this shit over."

"How are we going to do it?" Dave asked.

"I'm going to make them an offer they can't refuse."

"Like in *The Godfather*?" Brad asked.

"We all know how that turned out," I said.

"Michael took over everything," Dave said.

"Exactly," I said. "Let's start the takeover."

A week later, I got all the heads of the uptown projects. These were the people who thought they ran New Orleans. We sat at a round table in my warehouse.

"Why are we here?" Duck asked. He was short, red, and slim. He had wavy hair and blue eyes. He ran the Magnolia Projects.

"Hell, I want to know that too." Taylor, who ran the Melpomene, was brown-skinned, fat, and bald.

Bee, the head of the St. Thomas, added, "So what's good?" He was dark-skinned and slim with a low fade.

These were all uptown projects. I needed them first before working on the downtown area. "I have an offer for you guys."

"What kind of offer?" They looked around the table at one another.

"I'll get to the point. I can give you keys cheaper than what you paying now, and there will never be a drought."

"What's our part of this deal?" Taylor asked.

"Let me be your supplier?"

"You want to run the whole city?" Duck asked,

"I just want y'all to buy the keys from me."

"No, thanks; we're good," Duck said.

The others nodded,

"I'm telling y'all. It will work."

"Man, I'm out. You're tripping if you think I'm going to work for you and let you run our shit," Duck said.

Taylor and Bee voiced their agreement and walked out.

After they left, I turned to Brad and Dave and the rest of my workers.

"Look, I want everything dead. Down to their toes even. It's time to take over."

CHAPTER 39
Keith
2002

Shantell had been on my mind a lot lately, but I didn't have any time to talk to her. I was too busy moving keys. Also, I was at war with those nigga. I had too much money, so they were losing. I was moving drugs all the way up to Shreveport in Louisiana. I even had a few niggas from Mississippi coming to get work.

I decided it was important to make time for Shantell, so I had called her and ask her if she would like to go out. I really liked her and I was feeling her. She was different from the other females I've dealt with in the pass.

I pulled up in my new $150,000 black Corvette. She came out from her mother's house in tight blue jeans, a red blouse, and red stiletto's. She was carrying a red Gucci purse.

As soon as she got in my car, I saw she had an attitude. She sat with her arms folded and a sullen look on her face.

"What's wrong, baby?" I asked.

"Two weeks, nigga."

"You know I've been busy."

"Yeah, probably out fucking other bitches."

"Man, don't start that bullshit."

"Bullshit?"

"Do you want to go to dinner or what?"

"No."

"So what it do?"

"Go to your place."

***

We were naked at my condo. I was down between her legs eating her pussy. She grabbed my head, grinding her pussy in my face.

"Fuck, don't stop, I'm cumming," she moaned.

As she started to shake, I slid my dick in her wet pussy as she dug her nails into my back.

"I love you. I swear I do," she said as she tongue-kissed me.

I put her legs on my shoulders. I drove in her deeper and harder as I start to shake.

"I'm cumming, baby."

"Shoot all that hot cum in me."

She wrapped her legs around me as I came all inside her. "I love you too," I said.

We lay in bed and talked as I rubbed my hands through her hair. "You know it's about time for me to go back to school. What are you going to do when I leave?"

"Chill and make money."

"You're not going to come see me?"

"I didn't know you wanted me to? You might have a boyfriend out there."

"I ain't got no fucking boyfriend out there. The only man I've got is lying next to me."

"I'm your man now?"

"You've been my man since I gave you my pussy."

"Is that right?"

"Yeah. Besides, I ain't been with a man in almost two years since I met you."

"Why is that?"

"He's in prison. The Feds gave him ten years."

"I see,"

"I do need to tell you something."

"I'm all ears."

"How do you feel about bisexual women?"

"Shit, you like girls? I'm with all that."

"Well, I do have a girl I've been getting down with."

"Are y'all in a relationship?"

"Naw, we're more like fucking partners."

"So what's the problem?"

"Nothing really. I just want you to know. I don't want to keep secrets from you."

"I feel that."

"Okay, since I'm going to be your main girl, you need to let all them other bitches know that I'm the only bitch in your life." She climbed on top of me and put my dick in her warm wet pussy.

"I got you."

You know, I think I'm in love with this woman.

CHAPTER 40
Keith

I was driving down Washington near the Magnolia. I was looking for that nigga Duck. I was going to bust his head. I had Brad on Taylor, and Dave was after Bee. Since those niggas didn't want to play with me, it was time to put in work. These niggas were in the way. It was time to get rid of these niggas.

I couldn't sit back and let others do my work for me. I had to be involved personally. I'm a hands-on type of guy. I knew shit would bring in the Feds, but it had to be done.

I cut Trish loose. I told her she didn't need to get involved with the Feds. Moving drugs is one thing; covering up murders is a whole different animal. She would get life for that. Besides, I'd been kicking with Shantell more. She was about to go back to school. I was really feeling her. She had a different vibe and a good head on her shoulders. She wanted to make something of herself. The rest of those ghetto hoes I'd been fucking ain't got shit going on for themselves. They will always live in the projects. If I went to prison, they'd just latch onto the next dope boy.

It looked like I could make a future with Shantell. She reminded me of Candy in so many ways. They were both smart and beautiful and wanted more from life. Also, both had wanted me out of the game. I'd only known her for a couple of months, but it seemed like forever. She had some fire pussy and liked girls. Both are plusses.

Suddenly, I saw Duck at the red light. He was arguing with some chick in his red Benz. I turned my bike around and pulled alongside him at the light at Washington and Claiborne. He never saw me since I was wearing a helmet, and he was too involved in an argument with a fat black chick.

I pulled out a 9mm from my waist and unloaded them, killing everyone in the car, and pulled off.

CHAPTER 41
FBI Special Agent Jonathan Frost

I pulled up to the scene of a gang murder at the intersection of Washington and Claiborne near the Magnolia projects. I was with my fellow agent Paul Black. The NOPD had the scene secured with yellow and red tape. I figured that they were worried. After all, why would the FBI show up at the scene of a murdered gangster? There were two reasons. We needed to take over down here. There had been too many killings. More importantly, a CI told us that there was an ongoing drug war in the city between the Calliope gang head Keith Washington and everyone else in the city. It looked like Washington was trying to take over.

We showed our badges to the officers on scene and they let us through. We looked in the car. The victims had been shot multiple times in the face and body. There were shells all around the car. "What do you have, Paul?"

"Some bullet casings. I'm sending them to the lab for fingerprints."

My phone rang. I spoke briefly and hung up. "Let's go, Paul."

"What's up?"

"Another homicide. This one is in a warehouse."

We got to the warehouse and entered. A man had been restrained with duct tape. He had been beaten and shot in the head twice.

"Jon, this is the third homicide today. I don't think the vics are average citizens."

"We'll get pictures. Forensics can run them through some databases."

"I have a feelin these are guys who ran the other projects."

"If they are, we know it's that motherfucker Washington behind this shit."

***

Later, we were reading over the reports. "First victim is Terrell

Lewis, a.k.a. Duck," I told Paul.

"The guy from the car this morning?"

"Yeah, he's got a long rap sheet, mostly drug possession and guns, but he has killed people. He spent ten years in Angola. He's the most probable person suspected of running the Magnolia projects. Number two is Taylor Smith. The guy on the Lakefront last night with his throat cut and bullet wounds to the head with the woman dead in the passenger seat. Smith has spent time in Hunt's Prison for robbery. His rap sheet also includes murders. He runs the Melpomene."

"And the warehouse guy?"

"Corey Low, a.k.a. Bee. Same offense as the others. He's been in Angola. He was running things in the St. Thomas."

"Did the CI name the person supplying the projects now?"

"Keith Washington. He runs things in the Calliope with his fucking murder gang crew."

"We need to pay him a visit. I like him for the murders. If he didn't do them, he ordered them to do it."

CHAPTER 42
Keith

I was chilling with Shantell in my condo. She was going back to school in a couple of days. We had just finished fucking and were watching a movie.

My door came flying open. Federal agents and the U.S. Marshalls poured into the room, pointing guns at me and Shantell. I had been through this with the NOPD, but this was the Feds. I knew they were coming. I had Duck, Taylor, and Bee killed.

They let us dress before they put handcuffs on us and took us to the living room. They were ransacking my house. I knew they were looking for a murder weapon, but it wasn't here. I threw it in the river. I'm not a stupid nigga. I don't keep the guns I murdered people with.

"Man, do y'all have a warrant to tear up my shit?"

"Read it, motherfucker." The Marshall shoved me a piece of paper.

"What are y'all looking for?"

"We'll let you know when we find it," Agent Frost answered.

"Bingo." Agent Black came into the living room with a black 9mm Glock. "Take his ass."

"What about the girl?" the Marshall asked.

"Let her go. She doesn't know shit. She just one of the countless bitches that he's fucking."

"Man, whatever," I said.

"On second thought, bring her along. She might help us."

"Keith!" Shantell started to cry.

"Don't trip I got you. Man, y'all on some bullshit."

"Take them."

***

I was waiting in an interrogation room. I was worried about Shantell. She was probably scared to death. Fortunately, she didn't know shit. I didn't want her to know shit just in case these bitches pressed her. She wasn't built for drug shit.

Agents Black and Frost re-entered the room. They sat down and shoved some pictures in front me. I turned my head away.

"So you don't want to see your work?"

"Lawyer."

"Your ass needs one. We found fingerprints on the gun."

"Lawyer."

"The pretty lady told us everything."

"Lawyer." I knew they were lying about everything. The gun was clean. It was registered to my sister. I'd say she left it the last time she came over.

Baldwin, my lawyer, came in. "I've told you before, if you want to question my client, you have to come through me. So either charge him, or we're leaving."

"We're charging him with first degree murder."

"Don't worry, Keith. I'll handle this."

They put the handcuffs back on me and led me from the room.

CHAPTER 43
Keith
2002

The Marshall led me into the courtroom. I took it to trial. If I plead guilty, they were going to give me twenty years. They wanted me to name corrupted NOPD offices, including Trish, but I wasn't saying anything. They knew I had been fucking Trish because they had been watching me for months. They were putting me through this shit because I wouldn't cooperate with them.

Brad and Dave were taking care of things in the streets. I hadn't talk to Shantell. She went back to school. I didn't blame her. Way too much shit was going on in my life. I figured we'd catch up with one other later if it was meant to be.

I looked around the courtroom. To my surprise, Shantell was there. She looked good with a blue dress fitting her body right.

Baldwin turned to me. "How you doing?"

"I'm good. Any news?"

"They've offered a new deal."

"What is it?"

"No murder charge; five years on the gun."

"It ain't my gun.'

"I know. Just chill. When they came like this right before a trial, they didn't have shit besides the rationale for the warrant for the murder weapon. They didn't find it, so the case will have to be thrown out."

A slim white prosecutor came over to whisper something in Baldwin's ear.

"What is it?"

They called to order. The judge entered and started the session.

"Your Honor, may I approach the bench?" the prosecutor asked.

I was very nervous. I didn't know what the fuck was going on.

Baldwin came back smiling. He sat down.

"What's happening?"

"It's all good. Listen."

The judge spoke, "The United States has decided to drop all

charges."

I started smiling on the inside.

"Mr. Washington the court moves to dismiss your charges with prejudice. We're sorry that you had to endure this ordeal."

As I walked out of the court, I felt like John Gotti, who had beaten the Feds in two murder cases.

Shantell ran up to hug and kiss me.

"I thought you went back to school?"

"I did, but I couldn't miss your court date."

We went back to my place to fuck like rabbits.

CHAPTER 44
Shantell
2003

I was at Jackie's house smoking weed and talking. For the past few months, Keith had been taking me on shopping sprees. He had given me a new Benz. It was my last weekend in the city. I needed to get my ass back to school. I just took off for Keith's trial. I knew he hadn't really done anything.

I had finally admitted to Brittney that I was in love with Keith. She was a little mad. She didn't want to see me with anyone but her. But she was tripping. She had a man. I needed some dick too. I wasn't tripping. She'd get over it or not; her decision.

"When are you going back to Houston?"

"Next—"

Before I could get another word out, I ran into the bathroom and threw up.

Jackie came in, "You all right?"

"Bitch, I don't feel good."

"What did you eat?"

"Nothing."

"That's not true. You've been eating on Keith's dick."

"I'm serious, bitch, I don't feel good."

"Your ass is pregnant.

"I can't be. I've got to go back to school."

Jackie handed me a pregnancy test. I peed on the stick. I sat on her couch awaiting results. I was nervous as fuck. I had my ass, fingers, toes, and anything else you can think of crossed. I couldn't be pregnant. I needed to finish school. My mother would have a stroke if she found out I'm pregnant.

Jackie came in.

"What does it say?" I asked.

"Your ass is pregnant."

"What?" I jumped off the sofa and snatched the stick from her hands. There were two lines on it. I ran to the bathroom and grabbed the box and read it. "Shit! Fuck! Goddamn it! This shit can't be happening. My mother will kill my ass.

"Forget your mother. Will you tell Keith?"

"I'm not worried about him. I'll tell him. But my mother is going to kill me."

"I'm here for you." She was rubbing my back.

"I've got to go."

"Hit me up."

"I will."

***

Later, I was getting ready to see Keith. He still didn't know. My mother came in. I hadn't told her either. She didn't like Keith. She knew what he did, and she hated drug dealers. She had been wishing his ass would get time. She wanted me to leave him.

A few weeks passed. I was supposed to be back in Houston, I hadn't packed anything. I couldn't go back. I had a child to think about. I hoped this nigga would be there for me and my baby. Jackie wanted me to get an abortion. That wasn't an option. I didn't give a fuck about what could happen. I couldn't kill my baby.

"When are you going back to school?" my mother asked.

"I'm not going back."

"What? If you think you're going to live here and run the streets with that drug dealing piece of shit, you have another thing coming. Get your ass back to school."

"I can't. I'm pregnant."

"What?"

"I'm pregnant."

"Fuck, girl."

I just looked at her.

"You told his worthless ass?"

"Not yet."

"You need to. You can't stay here."

"That's how you're going to be to me and my kid?" I grabbed my purse and ran from the house.

"Shantell! Shantell!" My mother called.

But I ignored her. Keith pulled up, and I got in the car.

"Pull off."

"What?"

"Pull the fucking car off."

He did. "What is wrong with you?"

"Nothing. It's not your problem."

"What do you mean? Anything bothering you is important to me."

"I don't want to talk about it."

He pulled to the side of the road and touched my thigh.

"Why did you stop the car?"

"I need to know what's going on with you now."

I looked out the window so he wouldn't see me crying. "It's nothing."

"Are you crying?"

"Can you please drive?"

"Not until you tell me what's going on.

I turned to him. Tears ran down my face.

"Oh, hell no. Who did it to you? I'll kill their ass."

"You can't kill my mother."

"Your mother? What's going on here?"

"I'll tell you at your house."

Later, we were on his sofa. I was still crying.

"Stop crying. Tell me what's going on."

"My mother and I had a big fight."

"About what?"

"I'm not going back to college."

"Why not?"

"The fight was also about you."

"What? Why did you and your mother have a fight over me?"

"She knows you deal drugs. She don't want me with you. She thinks I'm wasting my time and life fucking with you."

"How can she judge me like that? She doesn't even know me."

"That's what I said."

"So why are you not leaving for college? You need to finish your degree."

Tears came down harder."

"Tell me what's wrong," Keith insisted.

I looked up and took a deep breath.

"Please tell me," he pleaded.

"Keith. I'm…I'm pregnant."

"Are you sure?"

"I knew you wouldn't be with me."

"What? You're tripping. I do want to be with you."

"And my mother put me out. I don't have any place to stay."

"Don't trip. You can stay here. I got you and the baby."

"Are you serious?"

"I'm not about to have my girl and kid living on the streets. But promise that you'll go back and finish getting your degree after you have the baby."

"Okay. I promise."

I kissed him and led him into the bedroom to let him make love to me.

CHAPTER 45
Keith

I was riding with Dave, collecting money from various dope houses in the city. I had the entire uptown sewn up, all the projects and neighborhoods. I had uptown flooded with coke. My whole team was eating well. I still had the cheapest prices in the city. I was fucking with niggas from five or six different states. Shantell was due any time. The Feds were watching a nigga, but they didn't see me do shit.

"Man, I can't believe you're having a baby."

"Yeah, man, and it's going to be a boy."

"Nigga, are you going to have him out here in the streets?"

"Hell no! The nigga will be a nerd. I don't even want him near this shit."

"You say it like it's a bad thing. The streets have been good to us."

"I'm going through shit so he doesn't have to."

"Sounds like you're ready to give up the crown."

"Not yet. I'm thinking about marrying Shantell though."

"Marry? Nigga, it sounds like you're trying to square up around this bitch."

"I've been looking into construction."

"What do you know about building shit?"

"Nothing. But I know I can't do this shit for the rest of my life."

"Well, nigga, I'm in this shit to win. If you decide to give it up, just plug me into the plug."

"I won't leave you hanging."

My sister called me to tell me Shantell was at the hospital.

"Let's go. She's having the baby."

At the hospital, I rushed to her room. They dressed me in a mask and scrubs. I went to her and took her hand. "Baby, I'm here."

She smiled.

"Let's get the little man out of there. I need you to push for me," the doctor said.

Shantell pushed hard. "Oh, shit, it hurts."

"Push again," the doctor ordered.

My son came out. They cleaned his mouth, and he started crying. The nurse took him to clean him off and to weigh him. She brought him back wrapped in a blanket. She handed him to Shantell.

"He is six pounds. Congratulations."

"Hey, baby, you look just like your father," Shantell cooed.

"What are you going to name him?" her mother asked.

"Keith Jr." She turned to me. "Do you want to hold your son?"

I took him in my arms. I knew I couldn't stay in the game much longer. I had a son now. I handed him to his grandmother. I took a red ring box from my pocket. Everybody's eyes - Jackie, her mother, Dave, and Brad - got big. I paid one million for it. It was a big diamond ring with the platinum around it.

Shantell started crying. "What's this, Keith?"

I got down on my knee and proposed to her. "Will you marry me?"

"Yes."

I slid the ring on her finger and kissed her.

CHAPTER 46
Keith
2005

I took stock of my life as I headed for Houston. Shantell was pregnant again. It was a girl this time. I had the city on lock. I was the man there. Everybody got coke from me. The murder rate in the city was sky high. Bodies were being found everywhere. After Katrina, things gradually went back to how they were in the nineties, when New Orleans was the murder capital. There was an enormous amount of money waiting to be made.

It was kind of a shame, but I was thinking about calling it quits. I needed to be home for my son and soon-to-be daughter. Shantell definitely wanted me out of the game. But she really doesn't understand how far a nigga is in and who a nigga is. I keep her ass green as the grass. If the Feds come back, she doesn't need to know anything. She still thinks I'm just an average drug dealer. She doesn't know that I am the man that runs shit.

I was still fucking Rena on the low. She says she's pregnant, but I know it's not mine. I still fuck that crazy bitch Trish too. She divorced her husband and always wants me to come be with her. The bitch is out of her mind if she think I'll leave my family for her.

That nigga Deloso holds meetings every month. He wants everyone getting work from him to be there. I've seen motherfuckers show up, but not leave again. This nigga is on some ill shit, but the work is on time. There's never a drought with him. I'm getting 3000 keys a month now. And it's pure; never been stepped on. But I got to bring this shit to an end soon, as soon as my construction company is on solid footing. I've got a couple of small city contracts. I'm bidding for a contract to build a new hospital. If I get that, I'm out. I'll leave shit to Brad and Dave. They're really running everything now anyway. I'm either at home or at work mostly anyway. I only go out for shit like this, or if something major happens in the city, like when we going to war with some motherfucker. The majority of the time, I never see the work; only the money.

I arrived at a gleaming white colonial mansion on the North Side of Houston. It sat on what had to be fifty acres. A bodyguard patted me down for guns or wires. This was completely normal here. Deloso trusted no one. My escort took me to a conference room. A huge mahogany table with large black leather chairs dominated the room. People from all walks of life surrounded the table: black, white, Latino, male, female, old and young. All wore suits and all were in the same business: selling drug for the cartel.

This was my fourth meeting. They could be held anywhere, but typically took place in this house. Every motherfucker in the room looked nervous. You never knew what to expect from Deloso. You never knew what dirt this crazy motherfucker had dug up. Well, at least until he revealed it. He had people everywhere, and there was no way to know who they all were. That's why I kept my shit tight.

Deloso came in carrying a wooden baseball bat while dressed in a blue Armani suit. He stopped at the head of the table and stared at the group. His bodyguard entered, blocking the door behind them. I had seen the look on his face before. Somebody's ass was in trouble. Someone was already dead. 1 never understood why a person showed up if their shit not straight.

"Somebody isn't playing fair." Deloso walked around the table, punctuating his steps by lightly hitting the bat against his hand. "Somebody has talked to the Feds."

He stopped behind an older white woman from Chicago. He cocked the bat back and slammed it into her head. He beat the shit out of her head and blood flew everywhere. He stopped to catch his breath, pulled out a gun, and shot her in the head. We all took a turn shooting her.

He went back to the head of the table. "Meeting is over. Keith, we need to talk."

I waited into his living room as he changed clothes. He came back in a white Armani suite. He poured us a drink. He sat down beside me. "What did you need to discuss with me?"

"I'm thinking about getting out of the game."

"Why? You making good money. I give you anything you ask for. You're my right hand in New Orleans.

"I've started a business."

"Is this about my killing people at these meetings? It has to be done to keep people in line."

"I understand business. But I have a family I need to look out for."

"Family is important. I see why you're considering this."

"But—"

"But no. Once in the cartel, we are connected for life. Nothing else - prison, family, whatever - can separate this bond. Well, unless you talk to the Feds."

"So, if I try to leave, you're going to kill me?"

"Keith, this is business, and you know too much of mine. I just can't let you leave. That wouldn't be good for me."

I jumped up and stared at him. "After all the coke I moved for you, you would kill me?"

He arose. "Keith this is business. You wanted to run with the big dogs. This is the price."

"I put in my work."

"Work is never over."

"Exactly what are you saying?"

"I'll see what I can do. You have been good to never fuck me on a deal. Find someone in New Orleans to replace you - and I'm not talking some bullshit motherfucker. It needs to be someone you trust. Even out, you're responsible for his actions. He fucks me, and I'm going to kill him, you, and your family. Consider it carefully. Bring this person to the next meeting. We'll talk about this then."

We shook hands, and the bodyguard escorted me to my car.

CHAPTER 47
Shantell

Jackie, Ke'shon, and I were walking around the mall to look for baby clothes. I felt like I was about to burst. I was at seven months. Keith was talking shit about getting out of the game, but he hadn't yet. On top of everything else, I heard through the streets that his ass supposedly got another bitch pregnant.

"Have you decided on a name yet?" Ke'shon asked.

"I've had some thoughts, but fuck that now. I want to know more about the bitch."

"What bitch?" Ke'shon asked.

"Jackie, bitch, I know you heard that gossip going around the streets."

"I'm trying to stay out of y'all shit."

"Why? Bitch, you always in my business. Tell me."

"Them hoes' hair I fix says it some bitch named Rena. She used to work for him. The bitch was a C.O. at the jailhouse when he was in jail the first time."

"I don't give a fuck. So, he was sleeping with her with me pregnant?"

"I don't know."

"Is the bitch really pregnant?"

"The last time I saw her, she had a bump."

"I feel like I'm about to go insane.'

"Please don't. I told your ass before you started fucking with him. Where is Keith at?"

"Out of town. Houston. But I got something for his ass when he gets back."

"Bitch, I don't know why you even mad."

"This nigga cheated on me while I was pregnant."

"News flash: Keith had hoes way before you married him."

"I'm surprised he doesn't have more kids out there," Ke'shon said.

"Bitch, you know the type of nigga you're dealing with. Don't play dumb."

"He told me he gave all that shit up when he married me.'
"Just like he was giving up the streets, huh?"

CHAPTER 48
Keith

As I drove back on I-10, I had a horrible headache from thinking about what that motherfucker Deloso said. He told me that death was the only way out. He even said that even if he were to let me go, I'd be responsible for the new person. That nigga Dave was wanting to be the man so bad. I might give him a shot. Brad said he was leaving when I did.

It's just that Dave doesn't always think. He's too hotheaded, he always wants to go to war, but that fucks up the money. Deloso wants his on time. Dave doesn't understand that sometimes you have to let a motherfucker eat. You can't kill everybody. The Feds were still watching me, but I was on their back burner. I didn't need heat right now. I was trying to get out of the game.

Shantell had been trying to call me since I had gotten on the interstate. She'd been calling me like crazy. I hoped her ass wasn't going into labor.

I picked up the phone and she began. "Where're you at?"

"What's going on? You okay."

"No."

"Is the baby all right?"

"She's fine. We're not. We need to talk."

"About what?"

"Where are you at?"

"Almost home."

"We'll talk when you get home." She hung up,

I hope this wasn't no bullshit. I didn't need it now.

CHAPTER 49
Shantell

I was in the living room, pacing. I was hotter than fish grease. It's one thing to fool around while we were married. It's a whole other issue when he does it while a bitch is pregnant. But it's even worse to cheat and get another bitch pregnant. I guess I knew what kind of man I was marrying. I knew he was a dealer with bitches. But he told me he let those hoes go when we got married. I had to be a stupid bitch. I had been blinded by the money, the cars, and this big 1.5 million house in Eastover. But my eyes were open now.

I saw his car pull up into the driveway. I walked over to the door. My arms were folded. I tapped my foot impatiently. We hadn't been fucking - not in six months. My pussy was on fire. That's how pregnant bitches are. Our hormones are all over the place. A bitch has lots of hot flashes. And we crave fucked-up food. Mine is mixing chocolate and pickles.

I looked like a wild woman. My hair stood up all over my head. My clothes were only half on. My titties were bigger and nipples swollen. My ass was so big that it ate up all the boy shorts I was wearing. Right now, I had on some pink boy shorts and a white wife-beater. And I had a huge belly. I felt miserable. This nigga better not come in here and play with me.

I had destroyed the house. Shit was everywhere. Dishes were broken and his clothes were in the tub bleached.

He came with roses and candy and some jewelry boxes. "These are for you." He kissed me.

As mad and bad as I was, as much as I wanted him to answer some questions, my pussy had a mind of her own. It seemed like that bitch jumped out of my shorts on her own. He slid his finger into my shorts, making me cum as he finger fucked me. He spun me around, moved my shorts to the side, and slid his throbbing dick in my soaking wet pussy. He grabbed my shoulders, drilling me like I liked it. I started to shake hard and came like my water broke. Cum was running all down my legs. That shit felt good.

He lay on the floor and pulled me on top of him. He rubbed my ass as he sucked my swollen nipples. It hurt, but felt so good at the same time. I rode his dick like a champ. He started shaking while grinding my pussy on his dick. My pussy muscles pulled the cum out of his dick. His hot nut flooded my pussy.

We lay on the floor, trying to catch our breath. Though my pussy was still throbbing, my mind was fucked up. I couldn't really be mad at him right now. We could talk about that shit in the morning. Right now, I wanted more dick.

I sucked and licked it until it got hard again. We fucked all night.

CHAPTER 50
Keith

I watched as my beautiful baby girl was brought into this world. She was beautiful. Shantell was holding her. She looked like her and me.

"What are you going to name her?" Shantell's mother asked.

"Ka'wine. Keith, come hold your daughter."

I looked into her beautiful brown eyes. "Hey, baby girl, you're the love of my life." She seemed to smile at me. "Daddy loves you."

I knew what I had to do. I had one foot in the street and the other out. My company was worth twenty million. I needed to talk to Brad and Dave about what they wanted to do. I promised Shantell that I'd get out of the streets once our daughter was born. I needed to keep that promise.

Rena's baby wasn't mine. Shantell and I had a lot of fights over that shit. I'm glad it was behind us. I knew when I came home that night she was mad because her friends had told her that baby was mine. Also, I had been ignoring her, not fucking her like I should. I was busy. I was running my business trying to get my company off the ground and in the streets still.

My phone rang. I answered.

"Brad just got shot."

"What?"

"He was on his way to the hospital."

I hung up. "Shantell, I need to go for a minute." I got off the elevator near the emergency room. I saw them rushing him into the emergency surgery. It didn't look good. They were trying to revive him. Blood was everywhere.

"What's going on?" I asked.

"Sir, step away."

I watched helplessly as they rolled him past me to the operating room. Dave ran in the hospital and came over to me.

"What happened?" I asked.

"People say he was at the club arguing with some nigga over a hoe. The nigga pulled out a gun and shot him. They said he was hit three or four times."

"Where's this guy at?"

"I don't know. I got word on the street that his head is worth 50K."

"Make it a hundred. Bring him to me."

Dave left, and I paced. I hope my best friend would be okay. I told him he needed to stop hanging around the club, but the nigga liked hood rat bitches.

The doctor came out. "Is any family here for Brad Peoples?"

"Me. How's he doing?"

"We revived him, but he's still in critical condition. He's not out of the woods. He was shot three times. Two bullets hit him in the chest and the other in the neck. He's very lucky."

"Thanks, Doc. Keep me posted. I'm at the hospital. My wife had a baby today."

I couldn't believe my baby and best friend were in the hospital together. This started out being the most beautiful day ever; now it was one of the ugliest. I got back to Shantell's room. She was holding the baby and kissing her.

She looked up. "What's wrong?"

"Brad was shot."

"What? When?"

"A few hours ago."

"Is he okay?"

"I don't know. He's still in critical condition. The doctor is supposed to keep me posted."

"What happened?"

"He got shot at the club over some bitch."

"This is why I keep telling you that you have to get out of the streets."

"This doesn't have anything to do with the streets. He got shot at the club "

"You just don't get it, do you?"

"Not right now, Shantell. I have a lot on my plate right now."

"Well, your daughter is here now. Remember your promise."

"I know. I just need time to think."

"Think about your family."

I left and walked back to Brad's room. I wanted to break down and cry. I couldn't stand to see him hooked up to a machine and a lot of tubes.

"Nigga, fight. You can make it through this. You've got to come back."

I began to softly cry as I thought back to Price and Candy. Come to think of it, I never had told Shantell about that.

CHAPTER 51
Shantell

I was driving like a bat out of hell to Jackie's house. That motherfucker had done this shit to me for the last time. Fuck his ass. I pulled up, honking my horn incessantly.

She came out with tight green shorts and halter top. Her hair was pulled back in a ponytail. You know when black women put their hair in a ponytail a bitch is about to get her ass whipped. That's what was going to happen when I caught Keith with his bitch. He promised me that he was finished with her, but I knew better. I'd hired a private investigator. I knew where the bitch lived.

"What's going on? You got me up at one in the morning. You better have a big problem."

"That motherfucker thinks he's going to leave me alone with two kids while he's out fucking some bitch."

"You got me here over dick?"

I threw some pictures at her. "It's not about dick. The nigga's supposed to be my husband."

"What's this?"

"Pictures of him and that hoe I caught him with a couple of times."

"The police bitch?"

"Yeah."

"Where are the kids?"

"My mother has them."

"I told you he was a player way back in the game, but your ass wouldn't listen."

"It's too late for that I told you so shit."

"What are you going to do? Where are we going?"

I pulled up to a red brick house. Keith's black Bentley was in the driveway. "I knew this motherfucker was here," I said.

"Who stays here?"

"The bitch he's fucking."

"How do you know that?"

"I followed him a couple times. The same bitch always comes

to the door."

"Bitch, you crazy. Do you think she has any kids by him?"

"I don't know, and I don't care as long as he takes care of mine." I grabbed a wooden bat from the backseat.

"What are you going to do with that?"

"You'll see."

"Bitch, you're going to get both of us locked up. I knew I shouldn't have come with your crazy ass. Why didn't you call Kesha or Ke'shon."

"Those hoes were too scared to come. Besides, you're my best friend, and that's what best friends are for. You got to have a crazy bitch's back whether she's right or wrong."

I got out of the car, leaving Jackie looking nervous. But she couldn't say anything. I'd went with her so many times when she was dick whipped behind some of those niggas out of jail.

"Bitch, you're going to get us locked up!" she yelled from the car.

When I got to Keith's car, dogs started barking and a light came on in the nearby house. The bitch stayed in a white neighborhood in the eastern part of New Orleans. Keith probably bought the house for this hoe.

I started breaking Keith's windows with the bat. I pounded on the hood.

Jackie got out. "Bitch, you tripping for real. Let's go before somebody calls the police."

"Keith! Keith, get your bitch ass out of that hoe's house now!"

"Bitch, come on. Let's go now."

"I ain't moving a step until his ass comes outside. We all going to jail around this motherfucker tonight."

Keith came out, putting on his shirt. He saw his car and my bat. "What the fuck? You tripping."

"Nigga, you're in there fucking that bitch. I'm tripping?"

"Chill."

Keith tried to walk up to me. I tried to hit him with the bat, but he took me.

"Man, you're tripping, Shantell." He held me tight.

“Get the fuck off of me!”

“Who’s making all the noise outside my door? Is it that bitch Shantell?”

I took the bat from Keith and tried to run toward her, but Keith held me back. “Chill out,” he said.

“Are you going to let that hoe disrespect your wife like that? Tears were steaming down my face.

“Yeah, bitch, I’m fucking your husband. He eats my pussy every night.”

“Chill out, Trish.”

“Fuck that bitch!” Trish shouted.

Keith walked over and slapped the fuck out of her. All I saw was a wig going one way and ass other and her hitting the ground. “I told your ass to chill the fuck out. Go inside now.”

She got up rubbing her face as she went in the house. He came over to me.

“Shantell, please, baby. It’s not what you think.”

“I ain’t listening to this. I hope you’re happy with that bitch.”

Jackie and I got back in the car and smashed out.

CHAPTER 52
Keith
Two months later

I hadn't been home in a few days. Shantell was still mad at me. I broke it off with Trish. Shit had gone too far. She shouldn't have disrespected my wife. Plus, I had to put my hands on her. If I got to beat you, I don't need you.

I should have called it quits when Shantell caught us the first time, but went back to help her. After she got fired, she needed some help getting back on her feet. I give her a million dollars. After all, she had kept her mouth shut about me to the Feds. And she had an abortion. I fucked her a few more times, but mainly because Shantell kept riding my back about her. If she was going to charge me with it, I might as well get something out of it. It was over now.

I was afraid I might have to leave Shantell's ass. She was getting on my nerves with all this bitch shit. I didn't need to hear it all the time. Deloso kept asking what I was going to do, but I hadn't even had time to talk to Brad and Dave yet. I was taking care of that now.

I love my wife. I swear I do. But I have a lot of shit on my plate. I know it's partially my fault. I've never told her how much stress I'm under on the streets. I want to leave the game, but Deloso won't let me go. Dave wants it badly. However, I'm afraid he'll start a war with the whole city or get us all caught up with the Feds.

At the warehouse, Brad, Dave, and the crew were sitting around a table. Brad had been home for six months, but he was still walking with a cane. I'm just glad he's back. The nigga that shot him was sleeping with the gators.

"I'm calling this meeting to tell you I'm about to step down." I sat down at the head of the table.

"What brought this on?" Dave asked.

"I've had a good run. My company is up and running now. And I'm not in jail or dead."

"What are we supposed to do?" Dave asked.

"I talked to head of the Cartel. He will keep supplying you on the strength of me."

I feel a but coming on," Dave said.

"There is."

"I knew it."

"The catch is he doesn't want to let me out. He says I'm in with him for life. He's going to kill my family and me unless I find someone to take over. But there's a catch there. If you take the job and shit goes sideways, he'll kill you and your family as well as me and mine. Even if I'm out, I'm still responsible for who I bring in."

"Damn, my nigga!" Brad exclaimed.

"Fuck that. I want to get put down," Dave argued.

"Stop acting thirsty," Brad said.

"Nigga, I'm not thirsty. I'm trying to get my spot."

"Nigga, you're acting real crazy."

"You're just mad because you know he's going to give it to me."

"Nigga, you too deep in your feelings."

"What're you saying?" Dave stood up.

"Man, chill out. This is the kind of shit I'm talking about. My life is on the line. My plan was to divide it between you. I love you niggas the same," I said.

"I don't want the shit. I'm out when you're out," Brad said.

"It's on you, Dave. Give me a few days. I'll holla at Deloso and see what he wants to do. I'll plug you in with him."

"Okay."

"It's like this though. If you fuck me, best friend or not, I'll kill you myself. I want you to know this off the rip."

"I understand."

"Meeting is over."

CHAPTER 53

Shantell

Three weeks later

I was over at Jackie's house. We were sitting on the sofa in her living room smoking a blunt. We were talking shit, and I was feeling miserable. I hadn't seen Keith in a few days. I was missing him badly. I hated not waking up next to him getting some dick when I wanted it. Or just lying on his chest while he rubbed on my ass or played with my hair as we watched a movie together. A bitch was straight up sick.

He'd called a couple of times to see if the kids were alright and if we were straight. As bad as I wanted him to come home, I refused to be the one to break down. Okay, I admit I fucked up his car, and he had to buy a new one. Plus he bought us two Benz G wagons. His was white and mine was red.

I had heard through the grapevine that he was through with the bitch. When I left that house that night, I bleached all his clothes and threw them out, but the nigga didn't even care. He never even came home to see the mess. I ended up having to clean up the shit because of the homeowner rules in the neighborhood.

"Pass me the shit, please," Jackie said. "I told you that you should leave his ass, but you wanted to be stupid."

"Fuck his ass. I'm out this time."

"I'll believe it when I see it."

"Bitch, I'm telling you."

"As soon as that nigga comes knocking, your ass gone."

"You tripping. That nigga made a fool out of me for the last time."

"Bitch, you're dick whipped."

"No, bitch. I'm stupid in love."

"It's the same thing."

"It's not."

"So the dick's not good?"

"Bitch, I'm not saying that at all. But it's a lot more than just his dick."

“Sure, sure. But I’ll say it again: as soon as he comes knocking, you’re gone.”

“I bet you I won’t.”

“We’ll see.”

CHAPTER 54
Keith

I needed my wife back in my life. I was straight out lonely and depressed. I was tired of waking up alone. I even missed being woken by Junior jumping on the bed. I missed my family. I had fucked up bad this time. I called her a few times, but she didn't even answer for a nigga. I needed to get my pride out the way and face the music like a man. I loved my wife and kids. I knew where they were. She was at that nosy bitch Jackie's house.

I hadn't been home since that night. I was mad that she destroyed my car. And I was sure she had fucked up my clothes. It's just what black women do.

I was still undecided about Dave. He had been sweating me about it. Brad was right. This nigga was really acting too thirsty about this shit. I knew he could fuck something up and I would have to kill him.

I called Shantell for the hundredth time that day. She had been sending me straight to the voicemail, but she answered this time. "Stop fucking calling me."

"Shantell, we need to talk. I'm sorry. I just want you and the kids."

"You're right. You're a sorry-ass motherfucker."

"Please, can I see you?"

She hung up. I can't believe it. Out of all the bitches in the world I can have, I'm begging her to take me back. This is crazy. I must really be in love with this woman. And the reason why is because Shantell is not just another bitch in the streets. She's my wife. I married her because I love her. I was going to get her back.

I drove over to Jackie's house. It was midnight.

***

"Jackie, someone's knocking."

"Who would come here this late? I'm not expecting anyone." She walked over to the door. "It's Keith."

My pussy instantly got wet. There were butterflies flapping all over my stomach. My high was gone. As she opened the door, I smelled his Polo cologne.

"She's not fucking with you no more. Go back to fucking those bitches."

"Just call her to the door."

I fixed myself at the mirror. I couldn't let him see me looking like a wild woman. He didn't need to know I was stressing over him, even though I desperately wanted him back in my arms and my pussy.

"Whatever." She walked off.

He looked good - real good. I swear I felt a little drop of cum in my panties. I wanted him to bend me over right there and fuck me, but I wasn't going to give in.

"What do you want, Keith?"

"I'm truly sorry. I fucked up."

"I've heard this shit before. Why will this time be any different?"

"I let all them women go. And I'm backing away from the streets."

"You think I'm supposed to forgive you just because you're leaving that bitch?"

"I want to work on us. Whatever it takes."

"Oh, really?"

"Yes. And to prove it…" He dropped down on his knee and took out a baby blue jewelry box. Inside was a pink diamond in a 24 karat platinum band. It was bigger than my current one. A bitch was cumming for real.

"This is how you know I'm ready. Will you remarry me so we can start over again?"

I looked into his soulful eyes. "Yes. I'll marry you."

He put the new ring on my finger. The sparkle of the diamond damned near blinded me. I jumped in his arms and kissed him. I went back to the house to show Jackie.

"If it was me, I'd wouldn't have forgiven him. I told you that you were dick whipped."

"I'll call you."

When we got home, Keith and I fucked all over the house from sunup to sundown.

CHAPTER 55
Shantell
One month later

The plane landed in Los Vegas. We were there for our honeymoon. Obviously, I'd forgiven him. We renewed our vows, and everything was good. We took a SUV from the airport to the Bellagio, where we took the presidential suite. The motherfucker was laid out. A large bathroom with a big Jacuzzi with a big California king bed. It was easy to see why they called it the presidential suite. It had everything the President of the United States would need.

We got dressed and hit the strip. They had some bad bitches out there. Those hoes made me want to take one back to the hotel for a threesome. It'd been a while since I had my pussy licked, and Keith and I had never had a threesome together. I think I'm feeling freaky tonight. I might just bring a bad bitch home with us.

Keith had been real good lately. I hadn't caught him with any bitches. He'd been coming in at a reasonable time. We'd even taken a family vacation. He was putting in a lot time with his company. Shit, come to think about it, he'd been really good.

We hit a few clubs on the Strip. I wanted to go to this big-ass strip club called Sapphires. I heard there were bad bitches from all over in there.

When we entered, I was blown away. This motherfucker was huge. There was even a pool inside. It was packed from wall to wall with butt-naked bitches. Some were doing lap dances. Others were in the pool while others were dancing.

"Baby, this motherfucker is big," I said

"It's supposed to be the biggest in the United States."

"They sure got a lot of bad bitches in here tonight."

"You're not lying."

They had hoes from all over the world: black, white, Asian, Dominican, and Jamaican, just to name a few. At the bar, we ordered $20,000 in ones and bottles of Patron and CIROC. We sat at a table down front, where niggas were balling and throwing money. All kinds of people were here: doctors, lawyers, and of course, drug dealers.

Six hoes came during the night to give us lap dances. I went to throwing money everywhere. One bitch was Irish and Hungarian with a big ass. She was thick, had hazel eyes, and long black hair. I waved her over to us.

"What's up, baby. You want a lap dance?"

I smiled and she went to twerking all over me as I hit her ass with $200. I whispered to her, "Would you like to come by the hotel with me and my husband?"

She looked at Keith and smiled. "How much?"

"Two stacks."

"Let's go."

***

Back at the hotel, Keith sat back and watched the show. We tongue kissed each other and then sucked each other's nipples. I lay back and spread my legs and watched her going down on my swollen clit.

"Fuck, yeah. Suck on this pussy," I said, grinding against her face.

She looked up at me. I ran my hands through her hair and pushed her face back down into my pussy as I came in her mouth. She spread her legs, and I returned the favor. As I was eating her out, Keith came up behind me and started eating me out. As she came in my mouth, I came in his.

We sucked on his dick and balls at the same time. He shot cum everywhere. We sucked him back to life. He put on a rubber and fucked the shit out of me. I got in a doggy style position, letting him fuck me from the behind while he fingered my asshole.

"Fuck, yeah, daddy, give me that dick."

He slid his dick into my asshole. He gave it to me nice and hard, just like I like it. I had found out one day that I loved it that way when I was watching porn and slid the dildo in my asshole and fucked myself real hard and came back to back.

"Fuck. I'm about to cum."

"Me too, Shantell," Keith moaned.

She sucked my titties and watched as we came all over each other. We fucked all night long.

CHAPTER 56
Keith
Three months later

My life was going good. My company was doing real well. My marriage was off the chain. After Vegas, Shantell and I had a couple more threesomes. There was no reason for me to cheat on my wife anymore. I still had the shit with Deloso on my plate. He had called and wanted to talk. I told him I found someone to take my place. I had decided to give it to Dave. He wanted to be the boss of the streets so bad that I decided to let him have it. Deloso had told me to come alone to this meeting. At first, this made me nervous. It didn't sound right. He assured me that it wasn't anything like that.

I pulled up to his house. A bodyguard patted me down, like always, then escorted me into the house. Deloso was in his living room with a drink and smoking a cigar. He was dressed in a solid black Armani suit. He stood as I entered. I walked over to give him a hug.

"How's everything? Have a seat. Can I get you a drink?"

"I'm good."

"We need to have a short talk."

"About?"

"Remember the last time you were here? We spoke about you getting out?"

"Yeah, you told me to find someone, and I did."

"You have, but I've been thinking. I'm going to let you out. You got married and want to start a family. I believe in that. But I still need a plug in New Orleans. You've been good to me. Your dealings with me have always been straight. This is the least I can do for you."

"I've got someone in mind."

"I don't want to meet him. He will deal with one of my middle man."

"Okay."

"He's your friend, but I can't trust him like that. So he will deal with one of my men."

"Sound good."
"I wish you the best."

***

Back on I-10, I was happy as a motherfucker. I was out of the game and I don't owe a nigga shit. I've got my millions and family. And I beat the Feds. I didn't have to lie to Shantell anymore. I was truly out.

I called Dave.

He answered, "What's up, my nigga?"

"Nigga, where you at?"

"Out and about."

"Meet me at Anita's Restaurant."

"When?"

"In a couple hours."

I hung up and called Brad. "I'm out. It's all good."

"Have you told Dave?"

"I'm meeting him at Anita's in a minute."

"Come by my house afterwards."

"Okay."_

I pulled up at Anita's. Dave pulled in behind me in a white Bentley. He had on a blue and white Polo shirt with matching shorts and tennis shoes. He had platinum jewelry on his neck and was wearing big diamond rings and a Rolex. He looked like me back in the day. I only wore suits now though.

I walked over and dapped him off.

"What's good? Does he want to meet me?"

"No."

"Why not?"

"He let me out."

"What about me?"

"You're on, but you won't deal directly with him. Call this number when you need work. It's all good. Don't fuck this up."

"Man, I got this."

"It's all on you. You need to finish up with what we have and give me my money. Make sure you give Deloso his money. I'll finish this work, then I'm gone. There's 100 keys left."

"You don't trust me?"

"It's not about trust. It's business. I have to make sure he gets his."

"I feel you."

As I drove over to Brad's house, I had a feeling that this shit was going to go left. It wouldn't be long until Dave was dead or in the Feds. He was too hot-headed.

I knocked on Brad's door. He opened it and hugged me. We went to his living room where we sipped on some Jack while talking.

"Man, we sure made it," he began.

"Yeah, we did."

"We grew up in the projects dreaming of having a million dollars and being big time. Now look at us. We ducked the Feds and made it out."

"So you turned it over to Dave?"

"Yeah."

"Okay."

"I've got fifty bricks and two million cash in a stash spot in Slidell. Here's a key if you ever need it."

"You're really done?"

"I've got a family now, a good woman and two kids that I love. My company is worth 30 million, and I'm getting contracts from the city. It's all over for me."

"Okay, my nigga. I love you. If you ever need anything, call."

"Love you too."

"And I got that nigga's back."

"Please look out for him."

"I got him."

I pulled away from my old life in my black Bentley and went to fully join my new one.

When I got home, Shantell had the house smelling good. She had cooked my favorite meal: pork chops and mashed potatoes. My kids ran up to me. I picked them up, kissing them.

"I love y'all more than anything," I said before putting them down.

I went to the kitchen and kissed Shantell on back of her neck.

"Baby, stop before you get me started." She smiled and kissed me.

"That's what I want to do."

"I see you're happy to see me." She ground her pussy against my hard dick.

"You already know."

I took her hand and led her to the garage.

CHAPTER 57
Shantell

Looking around the table, I saw that I had everything I had ever wanted. My husband was home for good. He'd been here for supper every night since his last trip to Houston. All that drama in the streets was over with. Keith spent a lot more time with the kids and me. I was loving it. He gave me all the dick I could handle. If we kept this up, we'd soon be working on our third and fourth child. I was deeply in love with Keith Washington. My heart fluttered when I saw him. My pussy got moist. Every day was just like the first time I met him.

"Bow your heads. We need to say grace," I said.

Keith took over. "Thank you, God, for blessing me with a wonderful wife and kids. There's nothing more I could ever want. Thank you, Lord."

"Amen," the kids and I said.

I felt that our bond was stronger than ever. Nothing could break us. Little did I know our relationship was going to be tested in ways I could never imagine.

CHAPTER 58

Dave

One year later

I was at a dope house in the Calliope projects, counting money, and I had five bricks of heroin. I was the king of the city now. It was about time Keith got his ass out of the way. I ran this shit with an iron fist. I was hands on. I got in contact with the plug and told him I wasn't going to move coke. Heroin and pills was the new wave in the city. I told him I needed bricks of dope and bags of pills. I had a few young niggas on my team who were down to bust heads. I was at war with those niggas off 3 and G over the heroin trade.

I heard a knock. There were a couple of bad-ass bitches counting money butt naked in the bedroom. Two men were guarding the door.

"Who is it?" one called.

"It's Randy."

"Let him in."

Randy was wearing blue Gucci jeans, shirt, and boots. He was short and bald. I'd been serving him bricks and half bricks. He just came back from state prison. He'd done twenty years. I met him when I was doing time. He was running things over on Philip and Clio Street. He had shit sewn up around there. I'd been giving him bricks for 50K, but from everybody else I wanted 75K.

"What's up, Randy?"

"Nothing, cooling. You know me."

"What do you need?"

"I'm trying to get two bricks." He put a bag on the table.

"Count the money, Monica."

Monica was a fine-ass redbone from out of the Magnolia who I was fucking. She ran the money through a machine. "It's $100,000."

"Give him two bricks."

She put up two silver bricks sealed with red tape. That's how you recognized my shit.

"Good looking out," he said, dapping me off before he left.

CHAPTER 59
Randy

I walked around the corner and got in a black unmarked car. I sat down with two FBI agents as the car pulled off. I knew I was down bad for doing this shit, but they had me by the balls. I couldn't do life. I just got back from serving twenty. These bitches busted one of my workers, who gave me up. They raided my house and found a key of heroin and two AK-47's. I was looking at thirty years. So I made a deal. I had to set Dave up, and then I was free. I could even continue selling dope so long as I gave them a couple of busts every now and then. So I did it.

"What did you get?" Agent Thomas asked.

"Two keys. Like you said."

"Did you see Keith Washington?

"I haven't seen him in a minute."

"Is he supplying Green?"

"I don't know."

"There's too much heroin for Washington's hands not to be in the middle of it. We believe that his company is a front to launder drug money."

"Why do y'all think that? He could've just went straight."

"Not this motherfucker. You don't give up the whole city and millions of dollars to run a bullshit construction company," Agent Barry said.

"Well, we square, right? I did my part. I'm out."

"Motherfucker, you're never square with us until we decide you are."

"Man, y'all trying to get me killed."

"You made the deal: work for us, or thirty years," Agent Thomas said.

"What else do y'all want me to do?"

"Keep doing what you're doing. Tell us when you see Keith."

I got out of the car with two bricks of heroin. I drove off in my blue G wagon. I felt completely fucked up. But I really didn't feel bad. That's how niggas were playing the game nowadays.

EPILOGUE
Brad
Present Day

I went to the hospital to check on Keith before heading out of town. I hated seeing him all bandaged up. He looked so helpless. When it first happened, I couldn't believe it. He'd been out of the game for years and then this shit happened. He should have stayed in the game. I knew this between him and the cartel was not over with. He had sided with his wife, and she had told on them. Telling on them was a death sentence. I was surprised he wasn't in a body bag and toe-tagged in the morgue.

After I found out what Dave did to Keith, I had to get back in the game. I couldn't let everything we'd built go to shit. But I didn't fully understand this. When they found Dave, he'd been shot twice in the back of the head. I knew this was the cartel's work. But Keith was shot too many times. It felt like it was personal, not business. I have a reward out on the streets for information on who took the hit.

I had tried to call Shantell, but hadn't gotten an answer. I'd hire a private investigator because something didn't feel right. She should be here with her husband, unless she was already dead, and the body just hasn't been found. Or else she was involved in it. You never know about bitches in this city. You can't put anything past them.

I walked over to the bed and touched his hand. "My nigga, I'm here with you. I got you. I'll find out who did this and kill their ass. I give you my word."

I turned around and left the hospital, leaving my best friend behind me in a silence that was starting to seem never-ending.

The End

Submission Guideline

Submit the first three chapters of your completed manuscript to ldpsubmissions@gmail.com, subject line: Your book's title. The manuscript must be in a .doc file and sent as an attachment. Document should be in Times New Roman, double spaced and in size 12 font. Also, provide your synopsis and full contact information. If sending multiple submissions, they must each be in a separate email.

Have a story but no way to send it electronically? You can still submit to LDP/Ca$h Presents. Send in the first three chapters, written or typed, of your completed manuscript to:

LDP: Submissions Dept
Po Box 944
Stockbridge, Ga 30281

DO NOT send original manuscript. Must be a duplicate.

Provide your synopsis and a cover letter containing your full contact information.

Thanks for considering LDP and Ca$h Presents.

Coming Soon from Lock Down Publications/Ca$h Presents

BOW DOWN TO MY GANGSTA

By **Ca$h**

TORN BETWEEN TWO

By **Coffee**

THE STREETS STAINED MY SOUL **II**

By **Marcellus Allen**

BLOOD OF A BOSS **VI**

SHADOWS OF THE GAME II

By **Askari**

LOYAL TO THE GAME **IV**

By **T.J. & Jelissa**

A DOPEBOY'S PRAYER **II**

By **Eddie "Wolf" Lee**

IF LOVING YOU IS WRONG… **III**

By **Jelissa**

TRUE SAVAGE **VII**

MIDNIGHT CARTEL III

DOPE BOY MAGIC IV

CITY OF KINGZ II

By **Chris Green**

BLAST FOR ME **III**

A SAVAGE DOPEBOY III

CUTTHROAT MAFIA III

By **Ghost**

A HUSTLER'S DECEIT III

KILL ZONE **II**

BAE BELONGS TO ME III

A DOPE BOY'S QUEEN II

By **Aryanna**

COKE KINGS V

KING OF THE TRAP II

By **T.J. Edwards**

GORILLAZ IN THE BAY V

De'Kari

THE STREETS ARE CALLING II

Duquie Wilson

KINGPIN KILLAZ IV

STREET KINGS III

PAID IN BLOOD III

CARTEL KILLAZ IV

DOPE GODS III

Hood Rich

SINS OF A HUSTLA II

ASAD

KINGZ OF THE GAME V

Playa Ray

SLAUGHTER GANG IV

RUTHLESS HEART IV

By Willie Slaughter

THE HEART OF A SAVAGE III

By Jibril Williams

FUK SHYT II

By Blakk Diamond

FEAR MY GANGSTA 5

THE REALEST KILLAZ II

By Tranay Adams

TRAP GOD II

By Troublesome

YAYO IV

A SHOOTER'S AMBITION III

By S. Allen

GHOST MOB

Stilloan Robinson

KINGPIN DREAMS III

By Paper Boi Rari

CREAM

By Yolanda Moore

SON OF A DOPE FIEND III

By Renta

FOREVER GANGSTA II

GLOCKS ON SATIN SHEETS III

By Adrian Dulan

LOYALTY AIN'T PROMISED II

By Keith Williams

THE PRICE YOU PAY FOR LOVE II

DOPE GIRL MAGIC III

By Destiny Skai

CONFESSIONS OF A GANGSTA II

By Nicholas Lock

I'M NOTHING WITHOUT HIS LOVE II

By Monet Dragun

LIFE OF A SAVAGE IV

A GANGSTA'S QUR'AN II

MURDA SEASON II

By **Romell Tukes**

QUIET MONEY III

THUG LIFE II

By **Trai'Quan**

THE STREETS MADE ME III

By **Larry D. Wright**

THE ULTIMATE SACRIFICE VI

IF YOU CROSS ME ONCE II

ANGEL III

By **Anthony Fields**

THE LIFE OF A HOOD STAR

By Ca$h & Rashia Wilson

FRIEND OR FOE II

By **Mimi**

SAVAGE STORMS II

By **Meesha**

BLOOD ON THE MONEY II

By J-Blunt

Available Now

RESTRAINING ORDER **I & II**

By **CA$H & Coffee**

LOVE KNOWS NO BOUNDARIES **I II & III**

By **Coffee**

RAISED AS A GOON I, II, III & IV

BRED BY THE SLUMS I, II, III

BLAST FOR ME I & II

ROTTEN TO THE CORE I II III

A BRONX TALE I, II, III

DUFFEL BAG CARTEL I II III IV

HEARTLESS GOON I II III IV

A SAVAGE DOPEBOY I II

HEARTLESS GOON I II III

DRUG LORDS I II III

CUTTHROAT MAFIA I II

By **Ghost**

LAY IT DOWN **I & II**

LAST OF A DYING BREED

BLOOD STAINS OF A SHOTTA I & II III

By **Jamaica**

LOYAL TO THE GAME I II III

LIFE OF SIN I, II III

By **TJ & Jelissa**

BLOODY COMMAS I & II

SKI MASK CARTEL I II & III

KING OF NEW YORK I II,III IV V

RISE TO POWER I II III

COKE KINGS I II III IV

BORN HEARTLESS I II III IV

KING OF THE TRAP

By **T.J. Edwards**

IF LOVING HIM IS WRONG…I & II

LOVE ME EVEN WHEN IT HURTS I II III

By **Jelissa**

WHEN THE STREETS CLAP BACK I & II III

THE HEART OF A SAVAGE I II

By **Jibril Williams**

A DISTINGUISHED THUG STOLE MY HEART I II & III

LOVE SHOULDN'T HURT I II III IV

RENEGADE BOYS I II III IV

PAID IN KARMA I II III

SAVAGE STORMS

By **Meesha**

A GANGSTER'S CODE I &, II III

A GANGSTER'S SYN I II III

THE SAVAGE LIFE I II III

CHAINED TO THE STREETS I II III

BLOOD ON THE MONEY

By J-Blunt

PUSH IT TO THE LIMIT

By **Bre' Hayes**

BLOOD OF A BOSS **I, II, III, IV, V**

SHADOWS OF THE GAME

By **Askari**

THE STREETS BLEED MURDER **I, II & III**

THE HEART OF A GANGSTA I II& III

By **Jerry Jackson**

CUM FOR ME I II III IV V

An **LDP Erotica Collaboration**

BRIDE OF A HUSTLA **I II & II**

THE FETTI GIRLS **I, II& III**

CORRUPTED BY A GANGSTA I, II III, IV

BLINDED BY HIS LOVE

THE PRICE YOU PAY FOR LOVE

DOPE GIRL MAGIC I II

By **Destiny Skai**

WHEN A GOOD GIRL GOES BAD

By **Adrienne**

THE COST OF LOYALTY I II III

By Kweli

A GANGSTER'S REVENGE **I II III & IV**

THE BOSS MAN'S DAUGHTERS I II III IV V

A SAVAGE LOVE **I & II**

BAE BELONGS TO ME I II

A HUSTLER'S DECEIT I, II, III

WHAT BAD BITCHES DO I, II, III

SOUL OF A MONSTER I II III

KILL ZONE

A DOPE BOY'S QUEEN

By **Aryanna**

A KINGPIN'S AMBITON

A KINGPIN'S AMBITION **II**

I MURDER FOR THE DOUGH

By **Ambitious**

TRUE SAVAGE I II III IV V VI

DOPE BOY MAGIC I, II, III

MIDNIGHT CARTEL I II

CITY OF KINGZ

By **Chris Green**

A DOPEBOY'S PRAYER

By **Eddie "Wolf" Lee**

THE KING CARTEL **I, II & III**

By **Frank Gresham**

THESE NIGGAS AIN'T LOYAL **I, II & III**

By **Nikki Tee**

GANGSTA SHYT **I II &III**

By **CATO**

THE ULTIMATE BETRAYAL

By **Phoenix**

BOSS'N UP **I , II & III**

By **Royal Nicole**

I LOVE YOU TO DEATH

By Destiny J

I RIDE FOR MY HITTA

I STILL RIDE FOR MY HITTA

By **Misty Holt**

LOVE & CHASIN' PAPER

By **Qay Crockett**

TO DIE IN VAIN

SINS OF A HUSTLA

By **ASAD**

BROOKLYN HUSTLAZ

By **Boogsy Morina**

BROOKLYN ON LOCK I & II

By **Sonovia**

GANGSTA CITY

By **Teddy Duke**

A DRUG KING AND HIS DIAMOND I & II III

A DOPEMAN'S RICHES

HER MAN, MINE'S TOO I, II

CASH MONEY HO'S

By Nicole Goosby

TRAPHOUSE KING **I II & III**

KINGPIN KILLAZ I II III

STREET KINGS I II

PAID IN BLOOD **I II**

CARTEL KILLAZ I II III

DOPE GODS I II

By **Hood Rich**

LIPSTICK KILLAH **I, II, III**

CRIME OF PASSION I II & III

FRIEND OR FOE

By **Mimi**

STEADY MOBBN' **I, II, III**

THE STREETS STAINED MY SOUL

By **Marcellus Allen**

WHO SHOT YA **I, II, III**

SON OF A DOPE FIEND I II

Renta

GORILLAZ IN THE BAY **I II III IV**

TEARS OF A GANGSTA I II

DE'KARI

TRIGGADALE I II III

Elijah R. Freeman

GOD BLESS THE TRAPPERS I, II, III

THESE SCANDALOUS STREETS I, II, III

FEAR MY GANGSTA I, II, III IV

THESE STREETS DON'T LOVE NOBODY I, II

BURY ME A G I, II, III, IV, V

A GANGSTA'S EMPIRE I, II, III, IV

THE DOPEMAN'S BODYGAURD I II

THE REALEST KILLAZ

Tranay Adams

THE STREETS ARE CALLING

Duquie Wilson

MARRIED TO A BOSS… I II III

By Destiny Skai & Chris Green

KINGZ OF THE GAME I II III IV

Playa Ray

SLAUGHTER GANG I II III

RUTHLESS HEART I II III

By Willie Slaughter

FUK SHYT

By Blakk Diamond

DON'T F#CK WITH MY HEART I II

By Linnea

ADDICTED TO THE DRAMA I II III

By Jamila

YAYO I II III

A SHOOTER'S AMBITION I II

By S. Allen

TRAP GOD

By Troublesome

FOREVER GANGSTA

GLOCKS ON SATIN SHEETS I II

By Adrian Dulan

TOE TAGZ I II III

By Ah'Million

KINGPIN DREAMS I II

By Paper Boi Rari

CONFESSIONS OF A GANGSTA

By Nicholas Lock

I'M NOTHING WITHOUT HIS LOVE

By Monet Dragun

CAUGHT UP IN THE LIFE I II III

By Robert Baptiste

NEW TO THE GAME I II III

By **Malik D. Rice**

LIFE OF A SAVAGE I II III

A GANGSTA'S QUR'AN

MURDA SEASON

By **Romell Tukes**

LOYALTY AIN'T PROMISED

By Keith Williams

QUIET MONEY I II

THUG LIFE

By **Trai'Quan**

THE STREETS MADE ME I II

By **Larry D. Wright**

THE ULTIMATE SACRIFICE I, II, III, IV, V

KHADIFI

IF YOU CROSS ME ONCE

ANGEL I II

By **Anthony Fields**

THE LIFE OF A HOOD STAR

By Ca$h & Rashia Wilson

BOOKS BY LDP'S CEO, CA$H

TRUST IN NO MAN

TRUST IN NO MAN 2

TRUST IN NO MAN 3

BONDED BY BLOOD

SHORTY GOT A THUG

THUGS CRY

THUGS CRY 2

THUGS CRY 3

TRUST NO BITCH

TRUST NO BITCH 2

TRUST NO BITCH 3

TIL MY CASKET DROPS

RESTRAINING ORDER

RESTRAINING ORDER 2

IN LOVE WITH A CONVICT

LIFE OF A HOOD STAR

Coming Soon

BONDED BY BLOOD 2

BOW DOWN TO MY GANGSTA

CPSIA information can be obtained
at www.ICGtesting.com
Printed in the USA
LVHW081951130321
681462LV00005B/435

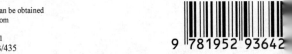